**Mal might not ever leave this place in his heart, naked and alone in front of a survival fire, unable to** protect himself from Tevyn's most outrageous whim.

Not wanting to protect himself.

Wanting Tevyn's attention on his heart, his soul, more than he'd wanted dignity, or safety, in his entire life of making them his quest.

# WELCOME TO

## REAMSPUN DESIRES

Dear Reader,

Love is the dream. It dazzles us, makes us stronger, and brings us to our knees. Dreamspun Desires tell stories of love featuring your favorite heartwarming heroes, captivating plots, and exotic locations. Stories that make your breath catch and your imagination soar.

In the pages of these wonderful love stories, readers can escape to a world where love conquers all, the tenderness of a first kiss sweeps you away, and your heart pounds at the sight of the one you love.

When you put it all together, you find romance in its truest form.

Love always finds a way.

*Elizabeth North*

Executive Director
Dreamspinner Press

# Amy Lane

## WARM HEART

PUBLISHED BY

Published by
DREAMSPINNER PRESS

5032 Capital Circle SW, Suite 2, PMB# 279,
Tallahassee, FL 32305-7886 USA
www.dreamspinnerpress.com

This is a work of fiction. Names, characters, places, and incidents either
are the product of author imagination or are used fictitiously, and any
resemblance to actual persons, living or dead, business establishments,
events, or locales is entirely coincidental.

Warm Heart
© 2019 Amy Lane
Editorial Development by Sue Brown-Moore

Cover Art
© 2019 Alexandria Corza
http://www.seeingstatic.com/
Cover content is for illustrative purposes only and any person depicted
on the cover is a model.

Paperback ISBN: 978-1-64108-213-6
Digital ISBN: 978-1-64405-543-4
Library of Congress Control Number: 2019934506
Paperback published July 2019
v. 1.0

Printed in the United States of America
∞
This paper meets the requirements of
ANSI/NISO Z39.48-1992 (Permanence of Paper).

**AMY LANE** lives in a crumbling crapmansion with a couple of growing children, a passel of furbabies, and a bemused spouse. She has finaled in the RITAs™ twice, has won honorable mention for an Indiefab, and has a couple of Rainbow Awards to her name. She also has too damned much yarn, a penchant for action-adventure movies, and a need to know that somewhere in all the pain is a story of Wuv, Twu Wuv, which she continues to believe in to this day! She writes fantasy, urban fantasy, and gay romance—and if you accidentally make eye contact, she'll bore you to tears with why those three genres go together. She'll also tell you that sacrifices, large and small, are worth the urge to write.

Website: www.greenshill.com
Blog: www.writerslane.blogspot.com
Email: amylane@greenshill.com
Facebook: www.facebook.com/amy.lane.167
Twitter: @amymaclane

# *By Amy Lane*

Published by **DREAMSPINNER PRESS**
www.dreamspinnerpress.com

Mate is washing dishes right now because I am so far behind. Tevyn wouldn't survive without Mal, and I wouldn't survive without Mate. Also, Mary seems to think this one is special—so this one, in its entirety, is hers.

## *Yearning for the Snow Bunny*

**MALLORY** Armstrong watched as Tevyn Moore floated his way through the ski lodge disco, stopping to dance with everyone on the floor.

Tevyn—shoulder-length curly blond hair flying, lithe, powerful athlete's body gyrating—had a smile and a booty bump for everybody he passed, and they, male and female, usually had a casual touch or a grope or an out-and-out caress saved for him.

He didn't seem to mind.

Mallory had managed Tevyn's money and his snowboarding competitions for the last five years, and he knew being touched was the last thing on Tevyn's bitch list. The boy was careless and free with that amazing body of his, and Mallory... Mallory just had to watch him, wondering who he'd find in the boy's bed tomorrow.

It was infuriating—even more so because Tevyn wasn't careless with protection or feckless with people's hearts. He worked in a physical profession. For God's sake, he did terrifying, death-defying things on a narrow plank of fiberglass, and he did them so well people paid him to wear hats with their logos on them. Someone whose stress was all physical was going to have physical ways to work that stress out.

Sex was as good a way as any, as far as Mallory could remember.

His last boyfriend had left him two years ago because, in his words, competing with Tevyn was too rough on the ego.

Mallory had sputtered then and protested. He was ten years older than Tevyn and was not planning to get involved with the boy. Tevyn was a *client*, one of a dozen who needed Mallory to manage their finances while they traveled to earn their money.

But Keith had laughed harshly and told him to save the excuses for the tabloids. Tevyn Moore dominated Mallory's schedule, his business, his life.

Well, he *did* dominate Mal's business. It was just that the boy was more than spectacularly talented on the slopes; he was also charismatic and business savvy. He couldn't so much as do a practice loop for fun without someone pushing him to sell their lip balm or skiing socks or even hair product. Tevyn knew enough to know he didn't want his name on a shitty product, but he didn't want to offend any potential sponsor, even one he had no intention of backing. *If only* Mal's other clients had the savvy to say no in such a way that they didn't offend anybody. Mallory didn't mind being Tevyn's fall guy; that was his job.

But Tevyn had learned to lean on him for matters that weren't financial—and that was a harder job altogether.

"Look at you!" Tevyn called from the dance floor, groin to groin with a young woman wearing basically a tank top that went down to midthigh and vinyl boots that met it at the same place. Mallory could tell she wasn't wearing any underwear under that thing, nor a bra neither, and her movements were as seductive and as rhythmic as Tevyn's.

"Look at me what?" Mallory called back from his perch at a high table near the edge, feeling awkward. He'd taken a helicopter out from the city in his three-piece suit and his loafers. He had sturdy boots and parkas and sweaters at home, of course—he visited Tevyn a lot when he was traveling—but Tevyn had been in the Sierras near Donner Pass for a private competition, and Mallory had taken the copter straight from his office. Damien Ward, his pilot, had been worried about a storm headed toward the ski resort and had told Mal that if they left tomorrow, they wouldn't be able to land.

"Look at you all serious!" Tevyn laughed, peeling away from the blonde in the uber-tank so gracefully it would have been impossible for her to take exception. "C'mon, Mal—it's an after-party! Find a guy and get down!"

Mallory grimaced at him over his scotch and soda. "Tev, I'm here for something serious. I need to talk to you."

Tevyn rolled his eyes. "Always serious with you, Mr. Finance Man. C'mon—I won today! I mean Shaun White wasn't here, but you gotta admit, that was some righteous air!"

Mallory had seen the half-pipe playback from the bar. He had dozens of clients, many of them high-end athletes and dancers, but God, only Tevyn could lodge his heart so solidly in his mouth. Up and over, twisting wildly in the air, he defied gravity with every jump. Mal had seen what happened to athletes who guessed wrong, landed wrong. Seeing Tevyn in the air terrified him.

"Righteous," he said weakly. "You were brilliant, Tev. As always."

Tevyn smiled prettily and fluffed his hair out of his eyes. "Then what's the problem? C'mon and celebrate with us!"

Mallory let out a wistful breath, wishing just this once he could go dance. Tevyn invited him every time, and every time Mal dismissed his flirting for Tev being Tev.

But God, to be moving next to that fine, strong body, watching Tevyn laugh like he had no cares in the world when Mallory knew that wasn't true—only once, he'd like to be the person with Tev's hands on his hips, the recipient of that billion-watt smile.

But not this ti—

Tevyn tugged at his hand unexpectedly, and Mal found himself face-to-face with his company's best, brightest, most problematic client.

"Tevyn—"

Tevyn wasn't that tall; many athletes weren't. He raised himself enough to put his lips by Mallory's ear and spoke under the relentless drive beat of the discotheque.

"Dance first, money man. Talk serious shit later!"

*Oh hell.*

Tevyn smelled like soap from the shower and like sweat from dancing, and, oddly enough, like wool. He wore a fine-gauge multicolored sweater over a white T-shirt and black yoga pants. Mallory knew for a fact Tevyn's grandmother had knitted the sweater. She knitted Tevyn one every year, right before competition season got fierce. Even Mallory had one, although Mallory's was plain blue, while Tevyn's tended to be in rainbow-hued colorways as opposed to plain colors.

Without thinking about it, Mallory found his hands on Tevyn's shoulders as they moved to the music, his thumbs absently stroking the fineness of Tevyn's sweater.

God, he didn't want to have this conversation with Tevyn anyway. Who wanted to tell someone that they had to make grown-up decisions because their grandmother was dying?

Tevyn grinned up at him, moving fluidly to the music, and for a moment, Mallory let his guard down.

Oh, this boy was pretty. He was pretty and graceful and so full of life. Five years ago Missy Moore, Tevyn's grandmother, had looked Mallory up on the computer, trying to find the best person to help a phenom manage his personal assets so the money would last long after his duration in a demanding sport. Tevyn wanted to go to college, she said. He wanted to own property in the mountains, because he'd grown up with her in a tiny town near the base of the Rockies in Colorado and would always want a tie to nature. He knew he wasn't going to be able to win championships forever. They both wanted him to be comfortable when he was done.

It sounded so simple—it was Mallory's job as a financial advisor in a nutshell. Another high-profile client on his roster. Hooray!

But things, it turned out, were so much more complicated than that.

Missy had been keeping up a good front for Tevyn, especially in the early days as Mallory had managed their assets and helped her keep her place in Colorado. But the truth was, her health was failing, and her memory was getting worse and worse.

Tevyn had hired nurses for her, and companions, and had pretty much worked Mallory's ass off to make sure she had anything she needed.

But as her health—both mental and physical— declined, Mallory realized he was the only person either of them trusted enough to say the hard thing, make the hard decision.

And now, dammit, it was time.

Besides the dreadful cost of Missy's care, which she had repeatedly insisted she didn't want Tevyn to pay for, although she had no money herself, the fact was, it wasn't safe anymore.

Tevyn knew about her spill off the porch and had even talked to her in the hospital. But Mallory had been there as they'd x-rayed her hip and had seen the congestion in her heart and lungs. He'd heard the doctors talking about the long recovery in the senior center, and he'd heard the words *congestive failure* and *quick decline*.

Missy wasn't going to be able to return to her home in Colorado.

Mallory was fuzzy on what had happened to Tevyn's parents. He knew from Tevyn's name that his father hadn't been a factor and his mother seemed to be a phantom. But whatever the history, Tevyn's only family wasn't going to make it through another competition season, and Tevyn needed to decide what to do.

And he also needed to see his grandmother one more time because they loved each other, and that was going to be the hardest part of all.

Mallory allowed Tevyn to pull him close with the familiarity of long acquaintanceship, and to lead their bodies into a lazy, awkward gyration. He ignored the heat and the pleasant smell of sweat radiating from Tevyn's body and concentrated on not stepping on his feet—and on the flushed crescents at Tevyn's cheeks as he tried to pretend he probably didn't have two of those of his own.

"You dance like a tree," Tevyn chided. Unexpectedly, he thrust his hand under Mallory's suit jacket and slid it around to Mallory's back. With a yank, he pulled Mallory's dress shirt out of his slacks before sliding his hand... his warm hand, rough and sure, right there. Right on the tender bare skin along his spine.

For an entire ten seconds, Mallory's body relaxed into that touch, and as he melted, Tevyn moved a little closer, hips swiveling to the music.

"Oh my—*Tev*!" Mallory gasped, trying to pull away. Tev wasn't having any of it, though.

"Relax," Tevyn ordered, winking. "Come on, Mal, you weren't this tense five years ago!"

Mallory thought about it, muscles easing unconsciously as he remembered Tevyn walking into his office, not quite twenty, Missy by his side. Tevyn had been wearing jeans and one of these sweaters, and had cracked a joke about finding a way to snowboard high enough to wave in the window of Mallory's San Francisco skyscraper office building.

Mallory—who had a lot of divas on his client list because he and his business partner, Charlie, really only took high-end athletes in with the rest of a diverse roster—had been charmed. He'd commented on Tevyn's sweater respectfully. His own mother had knitted, and he still wore the hats and gloves she'd made him.

He'd looked at Tevyn and seen someone young and promising, and, judging by the solicitous way he helped his grandmother sit down and got her a glass of water, more considerate than his usual clients.

Of course he'd relaxed.

Tevyn had just been so disarming.

And Tevyn hadn't changed at all in the five years since. He'd racked up four World Championships and three Olympic medals as well as a number of X Games victories and wins at countless smaller venues, but that charm, that joy, that bone-deep kindness hadn't faded in the least.

Mallory had been the one who'd changed.

In the second year, right before the Olympic Games, Tevyn had fallen and sprained his wrist. Mallory had been there—he wasn't always, but it was the Olympics, and hey, an excuse to go see cute guys perform amazing feats, right? But he'd been there as Tevyn had asked the doctor, very politely, the faintest hint of Colorado twang in his voice, to wrap his wrist tight so they could put a cast on it after the Olympic Games. The cast might alter his center of balance, he'd explained, and he really didn't want to fall on his head.

Every moment of the next three days, right up until Tevyn had stood on the podium, had been fraught with tension after that. Maybe because Mallory knew—not many other people did—and Mallory could see how much pain Tevyn had been in, had seen him push himself, cold sweat beading on his brow on the trip up the hill. Mallory had been the one to call Missy and reassure her that he was okay.

He'd lied because he knew the one unforgivable thing would be to get in the way of Tevyn making the next run.

Tevyn had medaled in three events, one of them a gold.

And then, when he'd gotten off the final podium, he'd gone to his group of supporters—Mallory among them—and asked, in a small voice, if they could help him get somewhere private. He needed to throw up.

Mallory had held his head, had called the doctor to give him an injection for the pain, had sat with him as he'd gotten X-rays, finally, and a cast.

All of the partying, the celebration, the camaraderie of the Olympics that year had washed right over the two of them as Tevyn dealt with the consequences of giving his body some hard use.

He'd been falling asleep, only half-lucid under painkillers, Mallory by his bed, when he'd said it.

"Don't much like pain. Winning's nice, though."

"You just let us know when the pain's too much, 'kay, Tev?" It was possibly the most fiscally reckless thing Mallory had ever said. Tevyn Moore was making him a lot of money, damaging his body for cash.

"Not the pain that's too much," Tevyn said. "It's the winning. Gotta find another rush, Mal. What's gonna beat this? Jumping off a cliff?"

"Don't you dare!" Mallory's heart hadn't been this cold since his mother passed away.

"Naw…. Missy would never forgive me."

"Maybe," Mal had offered, knowing how Tevyn lived his life, "you could try… I don't know. A relationship? Having someone next to you when you come down off the mountain?" He thought wistfully of his own history of mediocre relationships. He'd been with Keith at the time, had been making plans, but a part of him knew it was doomed. College, his job—nothing had ever been able to remove Mal's nose from the grindstone. Would certainly be nice if there was someone waiting for *him* when he came down from his ivory tower, right?

Tevyn had snorted. "What girl's gonna follow me around the world?" he asked. "What guy? People got their own lives, Mal. I'm just lucky I got you."

*I would follow you to the edge of the galaxy just to watch you make a 720 off the Crab Nebula.*

The thought, whimsical and unbidden, must have been beamed into Mallory's head by aliens. Mallory Armstrong didn't do poetry. He didn't do devotion. In spite of his mother's best efforts at theater and song, he didn't write Dr. Seuss books and only attended musical theater.

But that thought—that Mallory could devote his soul to this money-making freestyle wanderer—had sat in his chest even as Tevyn had drifted off.

*Oh God.*

*Oh Jesus.*

That thought was *true*.

*No no no no no*—Mallory was ten years older. Tevyn was *a client*. And Mal was… stolid. Rooted. He was concrete when Tevyn was air. How awful would it be to make a pass at air and fall into the ether?

Mal didn't understand how Tevyn did it every day of his life.

So Mal had buried that thought deep, deep into the bottom of his chest. Tevyn didn't need his pathetic old-man crush, right? Tevyn needed Mallory to be grounded. The sensible one. The one who minded his finances and helped him manage his increasingly needy grandmother.

So Mallory had resolved to be *that* guy for Tevyn, and it was a good resolution.

But he hadn't relaxed, not once, around Tevyn Simmons Moore since.

Until now. Tevyn's touch along his back was electric, and the music thudded seductively, and Mallory was so damned worried about Missy.

His body eased, melted, leaned into Tevyn's, swayed with the beat.

He became entranced by the solid graceful muscular presence that was Tevyn Moore.

Tevyn grinned at him, obviously delighted. "There we go! Wow, Mallory—had no idea you were such a good dancer!"

It was on the tip of Mal's tongue to say "I'm not!" and to back away. But this might be the last moment they'd have before Tevyn's life got really hard, and suddenly Mallory didn't want to squander it.

"Lots of hidden qualities about me," he said, swiveling his hips. "I'm a deep well of mystery."

Tevyn's laughter, his heat, all of it seeped into Mal's body, warming him, relaxing him. God, he might have to let Tevyn Moore out of his life, but he could certainly enjoy him now!

The drive beat ended abruptly, and the DJ called everybody to relax as the evening wound down. Mal stiffened as the music grew soft and sensual, but Tevyn cocked his head.

"Afraid of a slow dance?" He winked, and Mal's brain shorted out.

"Uhm…."

"Like a hug," Tevyn said, and because Mal was six foot tall and Tevyn was barely five eight, it was the most natural thing in the world for Tevyn to lean against his chest, and Mal to wrap his arms around Tevyn's shoulders.

*Gah!* He felt so good. And this was so wrong.

"Tevyn," Mal began hopelessly, not sure he could say this.

"Stop." Tevyn kept his head against Mal's chest, and the world imploded to only the two of them. "I know, Mal," he said, just loud enough for his voice to carry to Mallory and nobody else. "She's dying, and she can't go home. Her doctor called right after the ceremony."

Mal grunted, his arms tightening through no conscious thought. "I'm sorry. I—"

"You wanted to be the one to tell me." Tevyn sighed. "So kind. I thought… you know. We could have a dance before we went home tomorrow. That's all."

Mal's arms tightened even more. "Okay. One dance. I understand."

"No, you don't." Tevyn snuggled a little closer. "But maybe someday you will."

## *A Snow-Bunny's Bunny*

**TEVYN** wondered what it would take to get Mallory Armstrong to hold him like this forever.

Five years ago, he'd walked into Mal's office, feeling pretty damned cocky. He was one of the best snowboarders in the country, if not the world. He'd qualified for the Olympics when he was eighteen and could feel his body get better and better with every downhill run and every trick.

But nothing had prepared him for the razor-sharpness of Mallory Armstrong.

Tall, dark, handsome, with smoldering brown eyes and black hair that fell from a barely beginning widow's peak, Mallory had looked at home in his wood-and-chrome furnished office and blue pin-striped suit.

But as soon as he'd seen Tevyn's Grandma Missy, some of that sharpness had faded, and the man left had been solicitous and kind.

He'd taken every dollar Tevyn had made after that and applied it to things that meant the most to Tevyn and his grandmother, and he'd showed up at Tevyn's events because Missy couldn't.

Tevyn knew Mal did that for other clients, and for the first couple of years, he could brush away that sort of smug feeling of pride that burned in his stomach when he saw Mal—wearing dark blue Gore-Tex and bright orange wool as sort of the snow bunny's pinstripe—standing quietly with Tevyn's agent and trainer and physical therapist. Mal hung back, of course. He had no official standing at Tevyn's events. But Tevyn wanted him there, had told Sean Murphy, his agent, Gretta Klein, his trainer, and Harold Neil, his PT, that Mal was part of the team.

It was true. If Mal hadn't been part of the team, Tevyn and Missy would never have figured out how to afford a physical therapist and a trainer, and Mal had been the one to fire Tevyn's first agent, who had showed up to nothing and had done nothing to help land Tevyn endorsements.

But sometime after he'd broken his wrist, Tevyn had started taking a good look at Mal's calendar, and he'd realized Mallory Armstrong went to as many of Tevyn's events as he possibly could, while he made maybe two events a year for the other clients on his roster.

Tevyn would never put Mal on the spot about it, but he knew.

Mal thought he was special.

And coming out to tell Tevyn about his grandmother was a kindness.

Unlike a lot of the athletes on the snowboarding circuit, Tevyn had a home. He'd gone back to the cabin he'd grown up in as often as he could in the last five years, spending summers fixing it up between rock climbing and parkour in the mountains to keep fit. He'd known Missy wasn't what she had been when he was a kid. But he'd been doing a promotional surfing event in Australia at the end of this summer, and his week with Missy hadn't prepared him for the decline she'd had during his month away.

He'd started to prepare with Mallory then. More than just a companion who visited every day, they'd hired a nurse and set up an on-call service with a helicopter transport in case of emergency.

And still, every time Tevyn returned home, he'd had to spend a good two hours explaining to Missy where he'd been and why he looked so grown-up.

He hadn't been prepared for the doctor's phone call. And hadn't been prepared for the slug of need to his gut when he'd seen Mallory making his way through the disco after having arrived by helicopter shortly beforehand.

He hadn't been scheduled to be here.

He'd come anyway.

Tevyn held tight to him as the slow song wound down, taking in his cologne, the familiar wool of his coat, the crispness of his fine cotton shirt. Mal had lean lips and a quiet smile in the best of times, but now he was looking down at Tevyn from brown eyes that usually looked flinty with calculation.

Tonight they were warm with compassion.

"Song's over," Mallory rasped, and Tevyn took a reluctant step back.

Time to face the music.

**"DO** you have a room?" Tevyn asked as they both cleared the discotheque and made their way toward their lodgings. "I've got a suite. Gretta and Sean left after the event. Gretta was going to meet me at the qualifying rounds in Aspen in a month, and Hal is leaving tomorrow."

"I was going to leave tonight," Mallory began, but Tevyn shook his head with authority.

"I'd ask Damie about that. Visibility is going to be crap tonight. Snow's probably already started to fall. Tomorrow it should lighten up, but right now it's too dangerous."

Mal groaned. "Dammit! Dammit. I told Missy I'd try to get you there as soon as—"

Tevyn turned in the hall and touched him briefly on the arm, ignoring the charge that rippled up his back as he did. "Mallory, don't be dense. If Missy was in her right mind, she never would have told you to bring me back on a dime. She grew up in snow, and the winds in the mountains are fierce, I don't care if they're the Sierras or the Rockies. Now text Damie so he can stop shitting his pants and tell him to bring his go bag to my room."

Tevyn gave his room number and steered Mal down the hall toward the elevators, waving briefly to a couple of people he passed in the hallway.

"Friends?" Mal asked after he'd put his phone back in his pocket.

Tevyn shrugged and gave his "not really friends in bed" smile, and Mal's uncomfortable glance away was his reward.

He let out a bark of laughter then, trying not to be bitter. He wouldn't apologize for the people he'd been with during his years on the circuit, but he could admit that the number wasn't small.

So Mal's next words surprised him.

"I don't know how you do that," he said, shaking his head.

"Wave flirtily? It's an art form. I'll hold a class."

Mal's stolid grunt was reassuring. "No. How you can be on such good terms with everybody afterward. I had one boyfriend in five years, and he would literally set fire to a trash can for an excuse to walk on the other side of the road from me, and you sleep with beautiful people left and right, and they just... smile and wave."

Tevyn rolled his eyes and shook his head. "'Cause your one boyfriend was important," he explained, feeling like it was obvious. "So whatever broke you up, it hurt him. These guys—"

"And girls," Mal filled in sourly.

"And girls—they're, you know, dance partners who got naked."

"Is that why you wanted me to dance tonight?"

*Ouch.* "Don't be an ass. Do you have luggage, or did you leave from the office?" Tevyn hit the elevator button and wished for this conversation to be over. In the harsh light of the hallway, Mallory Armstrong was as calculating as he'd ever been, and the way he saw Tevyn was still as unflattering.

"I left from the office," Mal said, looking sheepish, and Tevyn's flare of temper passed. No luggage—he hopped in the company copter and went. That said something.

"Harold'll have something you can wear," he muttered, getting on the elevator and knowing Mal would follow. "And you and Damien can have Gretta's and Sean's beds." Tevyn scrubbed at his face, wishing—not for the first time—that Mal would just put that big autocratic hand on his shoulder, lower his head, and murmur, "We can share a bed."

But what good would that do?

Mal, the one solid presence in his life, would be reduced to a bedmate, and Tevyn would still be alone when he woke up in the morning.

"Thank you," Mallory said. "I didn't think beyond getting here to tell you."

Tevyn gave him a lopsided smile. "That's not like you. You usually plan three steps ahead." Tevyn had once seen Mal's open suitcase as he'd been packing to return home. The man had little carrying cases for everything—his ties, his gloves, his belts, his sweaters. It all fit together like a big wooden puzzle made of clothes and shoes.

"I was… anxious," Mal said. The door opened, and Tevyn led the way down the hall. "You're holding up very well, though."

Tevyn's smile turned hard while pulling out his key card. "Sure I am."

He moved to open the door to his suite, only to be stopped by Mal's hand on his. "Are you?"

Tevyn took a deep breath. "She raised me from a little kid, Mal. Mom left and became a random postcard, and Missy was there. I…. She taught me you can't fight a glacier or an avalanche, and shaking your fist at the snow is pure foolishness. But even if you can't stop it, that doesn't mean it won't freeze you, grind you, or tumble you about until you can fight clear."

Mal made a sound of sympathy, and Tevyn couldn't look at him. He opened the door to the suite and gestured in.

Harold Neil, Tevyn's physical therapist, was sprawled on the couch in front of the television in a way designed to send the healthiest back into spasms. A giant of a man—taller than Mal or even Damie, the helicopter pilot—Harold had dark clay-colored skin and wore his gray curls in a stout brush cut. He was twice divorced, in his fifties, and happy to, as he said, spend his years before retirement chasing Tevyn from snowfall to snowfall with the occasional foray to surf.

His whole regimen depended on Tevyn stretching at every opportunity, and an hour a day on the yoga mat was part of Tev's job.

"Hal?" Tevyn said softly, trying not to make the wake-up too rude. "Hal? You up?"

Harold choked on a snore and flailed off the couch, and on any other day, Tevyn would have been cracking up and throwing couch cushions at him while he flailed.

But it had actually been a hell of a day, and Tevyn could only manage a small smile.

"Hal?"

"Tevyn? Mallory? Tevyn, what's Mallory doing here?"

Tevyn kept his face still. "Remember that call I got about Missy?"

"Gah!" Harold scrubbed his face with his hand. "Yeah. You came to make sure he was all right?" His eyebrow arched skeptically.

If Tevyn hadn't spent that slow dance in Mal's arms, he wouldn't have been looking for the quick sideways glance Tevyn's way.

"Uh, yeah."

"He didn't bring any clothes." The adrenaline that had kept the sadness at bay in the club was fading now, and Tevyn found he just wanted to get Mal situated and go to his room. "If you could lend him some sweats, man, I'd appreciate it. Also Damie's on his way in—"

A knock at the door pretty much announced Tevyn's next item on the agenda, and as Mal went to answer it, Tevyn took that opportunity to disappear.

He stripped out of his club clothes and donned fleece pajama pants, an oversized T-shirt, and the sweater he'd been wearing at the club. It had been a toss-up between Missy's sweater and a hooded sweatshirt Tevyn had managed to steal from Mal. The fleece pajamas, bright and rainbow-colored, had been made by Missy the first year he'd gone traveling. God, he'd been, what? Seventeen then? On his own, getting laid a lot and blowing minds. You could get up a lot easier after a scary fall at seventeen than you could at twenty-five. Tevyn knew that he had ten, maybe fifteen years to do what he really loved at a competitive level before becoming a teacher and a footnote in snowboarding history.

The idea of doing it without Missy in his corner hit him like a fist to the middle. Oh man. He just wanted to see her while she still knew him. One last time, whether it was for a week or an afternoon. She'd broken her hip, and the doctor said infection often set in after a fall like that, and her heart had been going for years. She'd never been good at wearing slippers, even in the bitter chill of the Rocky Mountain foothills. She already had a cold. Tevyn was well aware her decline might be much faster than he'd imagined before the season had started.

With a sigh, he pulled the covers down in his bed, turned off his light, and curled up in a little ball, the better to vent his grief when nobody could hear.

He didn't hear Mallory enter the room, but he did feel the tentative hand between his shoulder blades.

"Wha—"

"Sh, Tev. Got up for water. Heard you."

Tevyn buried his face in the pillow. "'M that loud?"

"No. Was just… waiting. You were way too fine."

Tevyn gave a small laugh that turned into a hiccup that turned into a sob.

And then a curious thing happened. He took his own advice and just… relaxed. Stopped trying to fight the attraction between them, stopped trying to fight the intimacy. He gave in and let Mallory rub his back as he cried himself to sleep.

**HE** woke up to someone pounding on the connecting door.

"Wha—Mal, I'm getting up?"

"I'm right here!"

Tevyn was so surprised, he fell out of bed.

He was used to strange bodies in the morning, but never, ever, had he woken up with one of them fully clothed on top of the covers.

"Mal?" he mumbled. "Oh my God. You stayed last night?"

Mallory yawned and stretched, Harold's T-shirt and sweats flopping around his lean body. "You asked," he said grumpily.

Tevyn blinked. "I don't remember that." He'd said that? "I never ask anybody to stay." He'd begged his mother. He'd been six. That was the last time.

"Well, you asked me."

"Tev! Mal!" Damien called. "Guys, we gotta get a move on if we want to get out. There's another storm coming in, and if we don't hit the air in an hour, we're grounded!"

Tevyn hauled his hands through his hair. "Oh crap! Yeah! We're on it, Damie! Is Harold—"

"Staying here!" Harold called, seemingly from farther away. "I'll go get your gear and meet you with it at the copter!"

Tevyn came to his senses and opened the connecting door. They were both wearing pajamas and nothing had happened, and this "screaming through the hotel room" thing wasn't working. "Damie, can you ask Harold to get us some food? I'm okay flying, but you know me."

Damien nodded grimly. Tevyn needed carbs in his stomach before a flight. It was the weirdest thing, because he could do aerial acrobatics on an empty stomach for hours. But get him up in the air and his whole world went black without a decent breakfast.

"Got it," he said, then took in Tevyn's pajamas and gave Mal, still swimming in Hal's sweats, a look over Tevyn's shoulder. "Uh...."

"We were talking," Tevyn said with dignity.

"Frankly, I'd be more comfortable if you both were naked, but sure." Damien rolled his eyes as though he'd expected to find them naked for a couple of years. "Talking. Whatever you kids are doing these days."

Damien was about Mal's age, tall, fit, with curly dark hair, round brown eyes with a tilt at the outer corners, and tawny skin that marked Polynesian ancestry. Like Mal, he was hot enough to hit that, but, unlike Mal, Tevyn had only ever felt competence and warmth radiating from Damien, with no electric currents that made things like a dance or a late-night conversation awkward and painful. Damien was already dressed—jeans, boots, cabled sweater—and looked disgustingly perky.

Tevyn rolled his eyes. "Right now we're threatening death for some coffee. How's that? That radical enough for you?"

"Nice sweater," Damien snarked. "Did you shave a baby's ass for that sweater?"

Tevyn crossed his arms protectively over his chest. "Nobody disses my grandma Missy's knitting, you hear me?"

Damien laughed and ruffled his hair—because he *was* appallingly tall. "Get your fuzzy-butted sweater into my helicopter in less than an hour, or we'll get stuck in this suite for a week, and then I really might have to see you two naked, and that would be appalling!"

Damien spun on his heel then, leaving Tevyn to close the door.

"Forty-five minutes," Tevyn said with a sigh. "You just gotta shower and put on a suit." He gestured to the hotel room, which was in its usual spectacular state of disarray at the end of a competition. "Any ideas for this?"

Mal was standing and holding one side of Harold's sweats up so they didn't slide off his ass. "Yeah, I do. You shower first. Let me fold clothes. All you have to do is stuff your go bag, and Harold can bring the big suitcase later. Jesus, Tevyn, didn't Missy teach you how to pick up?"

"She tried." The clock was ticking, and Tevyn couldn't seem to move. They were standing across the room from each other, and all he could think was that he'd had Mallory Armstrong's heat at his back for the entire night, and he'd been asleep and unable to so much as rub his chest.

Mallory met his eyes then, and a charged silence filled the room.

"I, uh...."

"Thank you," Tevyn said, the words coming past a lump in his throat.

"For what?"

"Staying. Nobody but Missy ever stayed before. Thank you."

Tevyn watched in fascination as Mallory's throat grew blotchy and his cheeks filled with color. "All you ever have to do is ask," he said.

They both swallowed in tandem, eyes locked, as all the air drained out of the room. Damien shouted, "*Guys!*" and the spell was broken just enough for them to get a move on.

**FORTY-FIVE** minutes later, they were running out of the hotel room, loaded only with Tevyn's and Damien's go bags, and Tevyn had the distinct impression he'd left something important behind. Harold had strict instructions to pack what was left—folded into meticulous piles by the larger suitcase—and to drive them down to the city when he was ready to leave, and Tevyn's board and snow boots were already loaded into the small luggage space of the copter. The icy wind of Donner Pass battered at them as they climbed into the passenger compartment, and Damien's voice came over an intercom from the cockpit.

"The wind's picking up!" he called over the noise of the chopper blades revving up and the howl of the wind. "I'd say we've got about half an hour before it's over forty knots and we can't lift off. You guys okay with this?"

Tevyn met Mallory's gaze grimly. Missy could be around for another five months, but it was far more likely she would fade into unconsciousness in the next week.

"Go for it!" Mal called back. "If it gets too rough, we'll turn back. Your call."

"Deal!"

Mal opened a smaller compartment at the arm of the seat and pulled out earplugs and two headsets. Tevyn picked the headset, the better to know what was coming next, and made himself comfortable in the seat across. Both of them did their seat belts and glanced simultaneously outside, where the snow seemed to be falling thicker and faster now than it had two minutes ago when they'd boarded.

"Ready!" Damie said over the headset, and the chopper rose smoothly up, barely buffeted by the demonic wind.

Tevyn dug through his go bag and pulled out a protein bar from a box of twelve and offered Mal one. Mal shook his head, and Tevyn started to wolf down his own. God, flying. He was over the old joke that the guy who spent his living sailing into the air without a net and an engine was terrified of traveling in a helicopter. If he flew up twenty feet into the air on a snowboard, at least he could control his fall back to earth.

He crumpled up the protein bar wrapper and looked around them anxiously.

"It's getting heavier," he said, heart pounding in his chest. "I can't see the helipad anymore."

"I don't even know which direction it is," Mallory confirmed. A particularly brutal gust of wind caught the chopper broadside, and for a moment they swung, suspended by air pressure and the lift of the whirling blades. Tevyn's breath caught in his throat, and their forward momentum resumed.

"Should we tell him to turn it around?" Tev asked, covering the mouthpiece of the headset. "I meant what I said—nothing'll piss Grandma off more than us beating her to heaven."

Mal let out a short bark of laughter. "I hear you. We should trust Damie—"

"Had enough?" Damie called. "We're about ten miles out from the mountain, but guys, this isn't working. I've flown storm conditions before, but the crosscurrents and updrafts here are bigger than anything I've seen."

A huge gust of wind shook the chopper from stem to stern, and Tevyn didn't even have to look at Mal. "Abort!" they both called. "Turn her around! This isn't going to—"

The fist of God grabbed their helicopter, crumpled it into tinfoil, and threw it over his shoulder.

## *The Edge of the Cliff,
the Top of the Mountain*

**THE** world stopped spinning, and Mallory found himself sideways, suspended from his seat belt as his battered body dangled, looking down through the passenger window…

Into the vast nothingness of a snowscape far below.

"Oh my God!"

"Don't panic." Tevyn's voice, with that flinty Colorado accent, kept him from flailing. "Don't panic," he repeated. "But I need you to move. We're on the edge of the cliff, see that?"

"Can't see anything else." Down. Down down down, into a snow-covered gorge with spires of granite poking out like hammers and knives.

And the occasional white-topped tree.

"Well, stop it!" Tevyn snapped, and Mallory managed to look up to see that Tevyn had already undone his belt and scrambled up toward the door on the other side of the copter. "We need to get the hell out, Mal, and we need to get Damien out too."

Of course. Because Mallory was a hero like that.

"Absolutely," he said, his Mal's-got-everything-covered voice coming out of nowhere. Usually this was the voice he used with businesses that thought they were going under and had stocks that plummeted to the basement.

He'd never once used this voice when lives were at stake, but suddenly just pretending he had everything covered made it true.

Using a whole lot of Pilates, he maneuvered his body as though he were sitting, took the pressure off the seat belt, and hit the catch. He supported himself with his arm over the back of the seat, and by the time he'd clambered upward, Tevyn had managed to unlock the side door and—against all laws of gravity—push it open.

The frigid air blowing thick, wet snow into the compartment was a dire warning that surviving the crash was only the first part.

"Can you make it out?" Tevyn called. "I'm gonna check on Damie!"

Mal nodded grimly and ignored the ominous shudder as a gust of wind hit the helicopter and it shook, moving on the slushy snow.

From what he'd seen looking down, they were on the downward slope of a sharp cliff—and perilously close to the edge. If they didn't get Damien out of the cockpit quickly, they'd all go tumbling into the gorge.

Mal gasped as he pushed himself out into the lung-stopping cold, and his hands hurt immediately. *Shit!* He was still wearing his overcoat, and he scrambled in the pocket for the thin cashmere gloves he wore in the city. They'd get soaked quickly out here, but Tevyn was going to need some help.

Tevyn had been wearing his Gore-Tex parka and a hat, scarf, and sweater knit by Missy herself. Mal would put money down on him having gloves in the pocket, but Tevyn had grown up in the Rocky Mountains. His hands were inured to the cold, and he was struggling with the latch to the pilot's compartment as Mallory got in position to help him.

"Here!" he called. He had his house key, of all things, in his overcoat, and he pulled it out and knelt on the slippery metal hull, surprised the wind didn't just push him and Tevyn out into the canyon, it battered them so fiercely.

Tevyn saw what he was doing and pulled at the catch again, giving Mal a chance to pry at the stuck part with his key. The key shattered, and Mal struggled to catch himself at the same time Tevyn gave the latch a mighty yank, almost tumbling backward when it gave. Mal reached out a quick hand, terrified. Tevyn had his back to the canyon. One wrong move and he would have gone over, and Mal's heart fully stopped beating until Tevyn grabbed his hand.

"Quick thinking," he said with a tight grin. "Thanks."

Then he stretched out on the hull, bending at the waist to reach into the copter. "Damie!" he called. "Damie! Dammit, we gotta get out of here! Can you move?"

Damien's next words were mostly curses—Mal caught a burst of "goddamned updrafts" coupled with "spun me like a top" and ending with "motherfucking leg!"

Tevyn pushed up and looked at Mal seriously. "You need to help me haul him out of here and then get down to catch him. Normally I'd say tend to the leg first— bone's through the skin and it's pretty bad, but…."

Mal nodded. Neither of them wanted to say it. The fact was, they had a very limited time on that cliff slope before the helicopter slid off and fell into the canyon below.

"Go. I'll haul him up."

"He's gonna scream," Tevyn said soberly. "It's gonna hurt. Just remember, he knows why we're doing this, and we all want to get down this mountain. Deal?"

Mallory nodded and swallowed, wondering what hard experience Tevyn had with injuries and blizzard conditions to give him that certainty. He didn't ask, though. He just made sure his body was closer to the mountain than the canyon, to counterbalance whatever Tevyn was doing in the cockpit that made the whole helicopter tremble and groan.

Mal was shaking with cold, his jaw clenched from keeping his teeth still, by the time Damien's hands appeared as he barely supported himself. One look over his shoulder showed Tevyn lifting the lower part of his body from below, and Mal hustled in to help because Damien wasn't screaming—yet.

He bent at the knees, slick loafers barely giving him traction, and hauled at Damien's arms, and now Damie really *did* start to scream. Another effort, and he was high enough to turn himself so his bottom was on the edge of the doorway, and Mal looked behind him dubiously.

"This thing doesn't look that big when you're in it!" he hollered over the sound of the storm.

Damien let out a grunt. "Slide down the side and catch me."

"Will do!"

Mal went down on his stomach, feet facing the ground, grateful for the slightly higher temps of the Sierras versus other mountain ranges. The bad news was the snow was wet and they were going to be soaked to the skin very soon.

The good news was his clothes and skin weren't sticking to the icy hull of the copter—he just slid right down, caught his fall on his feet, and bent his knees to lessen the impact. He held up his arms and waited for Damien, yelping when Damie's big body came hurtling down faster than he expected. He managed to catch him by his shoulders, but momentum carried them both down into the snow, where Damien howled in pain and Mal struggled to get up, wet and freezing and scared in his balls.

It wasn't until he managed to turn Damien over and scramble to his feet that he realized Tevyn wasn't down on the ground with him. This side of the copter was relatively sheltered from the wind, which was a blessing, because the cold flakes had been stinging their faces on the hull, but as Mal steadied himself on one of the runners, he saw he had no visibility. He couldn't see how close they really were to the cliff, he couldn't see the top of the hull or the open hatches, and he couldn't see what the bloody hell Tevyn was doing.

The helicopter gave a long, shuddery groan because Mal had put weight on it, unintentionally, just by touching the runner on the downward slope.

God. He'd better get Damien up toward the peak, or they'd both go tumbling into the gorge if they weren't careful.

Mal got behind Damie and hauled him from under his armpits, his broken leg leaving a trail of blood in the snow. *Oh God.* Damien was going to bleed out if they didn't do something to stop that, and Mal thought about the arms of his overcoat and how they might use snow to make a pressure bandage, about how the overcoat might be used as a travois—but he had no idea what he'd do to survive if he took it off—and about anything, anything, but how the helicopter was sliding… sliding… slowly, now more quickly, and Tevyn was still monkeying around inside it.

"*Tevyn!*" he screamed. "Goddammit, Tevyn, get the hell out of there! What are you doing in—"

An object came sailing out of the passenger's compartment just as Mal got Damie up to the peak, where he couldn't slide down anymore. Mal dropped him unceremoniously, heartened by his squawk of pain because it meant he was still conscious. He made his way to the red thing in the snow and grunted.

A first aid kit. Goddammit. "Good job! Now get the fuc—"

This object was bigger, and the weight redistribution must have been bigger too, because the copter gave another groan. Mal trudged through the thigh-deep snow to the other thing Tevyn thought worth risking his life.

"Your go bag?" Mal called, looking at the large equipment bag Tevyn used for clothes and other supplies. "Okay. Fine. Are we getting your snowboard next?"

Actually that wasn't a bad idea. If he and Damie could make shelter, the snowboard could be Tevyn's ticket to go down the mountain and get help.

Mal hadn't even thought it before the copter gave another groan and Tevyn's bright rainbow-colored hat popped over the edge of the open hatch.

And the copter started its final slide over the edge.

"*Tevyn!*" Unconsciously, Mal started to slog toward the copter, toward the cliff's edge, toward Tevyn, who was hauling himself out by main strength and starting a perilous, tripping race along the side of the copter.

If Mal hadn't just slid down the side of the thing, he wouldn't have known what he was doing, but now he realized Tev was avoiding the runners on the bottom—and getting ready to leap off the nose of the copter, since the tail was leading the fall.

Oh God. It was going to be close. Mal watched, heart in his throat, as Tevyn took a giant step, then another, and then propelled himself off the nose of the copter in a leap that would have done a gazelle proud.

He landed on his knees on purpose and rolled, right as the copter gave a mighty creak and disappeared into the canyon below.

Mal stared at the open maw where their only means of transportation and shelter had disappeared and then at Tevyn, who was dusting snow off his jacket as he stood. He was wearing boots, and unlike Mal's footwear, they gave him some surface area. He sank a foot or so instead of all the way down past his knees. He practically ran to where Mal stood, shocked, holding a first aid kit and a go bag.

"You got 'em?" he asked, pleased and exhilarated.

"What in the hell?"

"There's a pressure bandage in the kit!" he said, still looking at Mal with that wide-eyed expectation of approval.

"That's fine. Why the go bag? What was in there you needed so badly you'd risk death to get?"

Tev's mouth set mutinously. "Not me, idiot! You and Damien! I got sweaters, water bottles, hand warmers, protein bars! If you think I'm getting off this mountain all alone, you're damned mistaken!"

Mal gaped at Tevyn, who stalked up the hill like snow and blizzards and cold didn't even exist.

Well, good for him. Apparently Mal's brain was frozen and useless, because dammit, Tevyn was right.

But Mal's heart wasn't slowing down. All he could think of was if that copter had taken Tevyn down, Mal might not have been able to keep from throwing himself into the canyon with it.

**THEIR** irritation at each other was forgotten as they neared Damien, wet and shivering in the snow.

"The tree line starts about a hundred yards from here," Tevyn said as he drew near. "We've got to get you both warm, but—"

"He's bleeding too much!" Mallory chattered. "We need to stabilize his leg!"

They met gazes tensely, and then both of them looked to the tree line, which was becoming less and less visible with every breath.

They looked at each other again and nodded. It was going to be close.

Tevyn reached into his pocket and tossed Mal a bowie knife. "Take off his boots and cut his jeans. Pack snow around the wound, and I'll figure out the bandage."

Mal nodded, opening the blade and sinking to his knees next to their friend—and thanking God for Boy Scouts until the eighth grade, because otherwise he wouldn't have been surprised if he cut off his own finger.

Damien let out a weak scream as Mal struggled with his boot, and then he whimpered and lay still. That made the rest easier on one level, but it was also disturbing on another. Damien was usually so quick-witted, so snarky—the silence was unnerving and urged Mal to greater speed. Their friend was far too vulnerable like that, head lolling in the snow.

The break itself was grisly, and Mal—who had never before considered himself to have a weak stomach—had to stomp down on nausea as he cut the denim around the protruding bone. By the time he'd laid the limb bare, Tevyn was at his side with the bandage.

"Crap, that's bad," Tevyn muttered. "God. Here's the thing, Mal. Moving him with that is gonna be a nightmare. I'd *really like* to reset the bone, but I'm not a frickin' doctor. I've had a lot of experience getting worked on, and I've paid attention—but *I'm not a frickin' doctor*. This is like a life-or-death thing, man, and on the one hand, we could pack the wound with snow and wrap it and haul him down the mountain with that thing sticking out threatening to sever a major artery."

"And the other?" Mal knew the answer, but Tevyn needed to say it out loud. Mallory trusted Tevyn—trusted him more than anything—but if Tevyn didn't trust himself, this was not going to work.

"The other is I pull gently on his foot and calf and see if the bone will at least slide back to where it's supposed to be. Then we pack the wound with snow and wrap it and haul it down the mountain and hope it doesn't sever a major artery or get infected and kill him. God*damn* it!"

Mal nodded and watched as Damien twitched and whimpered. "I trust you," Mal said quietly. "You know your anatomy. You know your physical therapy." Mal had seen him studying old injury X-rays while watching performance footage to see if the injury had impaired a movement or not. Tevyn was smart, and what the human body could or could not do was in the realm of his expertise.

"I do," Tevyn said. He took a deep breath. "Hold his thigh and say a prayer. We gotta do this now 'cause he's not gonna last, exposed like this. Let's go."

It took a surprising amount of strength, kneeling in the snow, and Damien's low, anguished moaning didn't help. But Tevyn's body was finely tuned, and his sure instinct for body mechanics made the final realignment possible. When the bone slid into place, they both let out a sigh of relief, and packing the wound and bandaging it was so much easier after that.

"Grab his other boot," Tevyn commanded as he was working. "I'm going to wrap his bottom half in one of the fireproof blankets. If we grab the corners, it'll be like hauling a really heavy sled."

"What am I doing with his boot?" Mal asked, teeth chattering.

"Putting it on. Your Italian loafers are for shit."

"I'm wearing shoes?"

Tevyn's unexpected bark of laughter gave him heart, which he needed, because his feet and toes ached fiercely. His socks had soaked through in his first five minutes on the ground, hauling Damien to safety.

"Do you have dry socks?" he asked.

"Yeah." Tevyn grimaced through the cloud of snow so thick they could barely see each other. "You want to wait until we get to the tree line?"

Mal nodded. "We're running out of time."

They were. It took both of them to secure Damien in his fire-blanket cocoon, and when they were done, Tevyn took his go bag and Mallory took the first aid kit, and both of them took a corner of the blanket. Together they walked, trudged, marched, and stumbled through wet stinging snow, which grew thicker with every step.

The frigid air rasped their lungs and froze their fingers and definitely Mallory's toes, and the wet snow soaked through his overcoat, his suit jacket, his shirt and T-shirt, sapping Mal's body heat and his strength.

But Tevyn was beside him, not giving up, and dammit if Mal was going to leave him alone.

*You stayed.*

*Goddammit, yes.* Mal had stayed. From what he could see, Tevyn's grandmother had been the only person in his life to promise permanence, and she was going. Mal *had* to stay, and he wasn't going to let a blizzard stop him.

The edge of the tree line felt almost like a lie, because the snow barely lessened up a little and the fringe of trees hardly provided any shelter from the wind. They kept trudging, looking for a rock, a fallen tree, anything that would give them shelter, give them some dry ground, even a windbreak that would let them start a fire and get their bearings and still the shrieking of the storm around them.

Tevyn spotted it first—a rough, rocky outcropping and a few trees close enough to form an umbrella along the edge. It wasn't huge, and it didn't have a heater or hot chocolate, but it did have some bare ground at the base where the snow hadn't been able to penetrate, and some trees to hang their other fire blankets from to serve as a lean-to.

They could get warm there, and that was a priority because Mal knew he couldn't keep going much longer like he was.

With a grunt and a lunge, they pulled Damien's tightly wrapped form into the small enclosure, and Tevyn took maybe a minute to catch his breath.

Then he dug through the go bag and came back with two pairs of wool socks, two of the homemade sweaters he always wore, and two warm all-wool hats.

"I'm going to fix us a windbreak," he explained tersely. "You, put this on yourself first—I can hear your teeth chattering from here. Then dress Damien—make sure you get his feet and then wrap him back up. The insulating blanket should have helped keep him dry, but he'll go into shock, you understand?"

Mal nodded because he couldn't trust himself to speak without chattering, and started to peel off his sopping wet cashmere gloves.

"Leave those on," Tevyn said shortly, taking Mal's hands and holding them between his own gloved fingers. "Wool actually keeps heat in even when it's wet—believe it or not, your hands will get colder unless we have a heat source. Change your socks. Get Damie squared away. Fire's next, okay?"

Mal nodded and gave him a shaky smile. "You are so on t-t-t-t-topppp of it," he praised. "I c-c-can d-d-do—"

Tevyn silenced him with fingers over his lips. "You're hanging in there like a champ," he said. "Let's get you and Damie warmed up, and it won't feel like I got all the answers. 'Cause I gotta tell you, what we do next is gonna need all our smarts."

Mal nodded, warmed emotionally by his
kindness, even if physically he was still a big frigid
ball of wet snow.

Tevyn gave his shoulder a little shove, and Mal
sat on a downed tree that felt like it was made to be a
bench, doing his best to follow Tevyn's orders.

The socks, indeed, felt like heaven over his aching
toes, but Damien's boots were a little big. Mal draped
his wet socks on the slope of the rock face, figuring if
they could dry off just a little, he could use them to pad
the inside of the boot.

Taking off his overcoat and suit jacket was a
misery, but once he'd stretched his way into Tevyn's
sweater.... *Ah, Gods.* He shuddered with the layer of
warmth over his body, and he put his suit jacket on over
it to keep the layers warm. Tevyn's hat was, again, a
blessing, and as soon as he was dressed, he sat down to
share the blessings.

Damien woke up enough to smile as Mal was
pulling on the rainbow-hued sweater and hat. "I'm out
of it for a little bit and you decide to decorate?"

"Glad you like it," Mal joked grimly. "Because
next stop is your feet."

"Oh God. No." Damien shuddered, and Mal
grabbed the first aid bag.

"Tevyn! Painkillers all right?"

Tevyn grunted and paused in the act of draping a fire
blanket over one of the biggest gaps of coverage from the
trees and securing it with what looked like spare boot laces
wrapped around the blanket and the branch. "Definitely.
You should both eat a power bar too. You need fuel to stay
warm, and you don't want to get depleted. There's three
water bottles in there—two refillable. Use the plastic one
first. I have an idea for that."

Mal took his directions, giving Damien two ibuprofen and wishing he had whiskey to wash it down with.

Damien swallowed the pills with a shudder. "Do we know our status yet?"

"Fucked?" Mal offered, and Damien crossed his eyes.

"Well, I asked. What's the plan?"

Mal looked around, thinking gratefully that the little shelter Tevyn had built had gotten a little warmer with the windbreak.

"Build a fire," he said, hoping they had what they needed to start one. "Wait out the storm. Assess the situation, figure out our options."

"I've got a lighter in my pocket," Damien said, and Mal almost cried in relief.

"You smoke?"

"No. Just lucky. Flew for the Navy, got it from my first flight instructor as a gift. Good luck. Hopefully it can save our asses—not that Grandma Missy's knitwear might not do it for us," he said with a grim smile. His eyes fluttered closed. "Whatever you were going to do with my feet, go for it. I'm fading, and I might be out of it enough to not mind so much."

He minded. He minded enough to squeak and pass out again, and Mal grimaced. Damie had worked for Mal's company a long time—they had a rapport, had sat down to drinks before. Damie had even hit on him once or twice after Keith, but Mal's stupid, blind, fruitless attachment to Tevyn had kept him from saying yes.

Seeing a friend in pain sucked.

But it did give Mal a chance to check on the circulation in his foot and make sure he wasn't bleeding too heavily into the pressure bandage. So far, so good— the foot was cold, but not frigid and not blue. Mal slid the socks on gingerly and then cocooned him again in the fire blanket, taking the lighter out before he bound him up. He bundled his overcoat under Damie's head, grateful for the bare ground instead of the snow, and set about snapping twigs and branches off the fallen soldier he'd been sitting on.

They were dryish. The tree hadn't been dead long enough for them to be truly seasoned, but with some pine needles and some paper they should start. While Tevyn worked on the lean-to, Mal left the shelter to gather more wood and was stunned by the force of the wind outside their snug little haven from the snow. He saw some dead branches about fifteen feet from the entrance to the lean-to and struggled in that direction, missing his overcoat again completely. He managed to grab the branch and was dragging it back, the better to stomp on it when they had some clear ground, when he heard his name called with a note of desperation.

"Mal? *Mallory*!"

"Right here!" he called back, pulling within sight of the opening. "Getting firewood. This should—"

"You got to tell me!" Tevyn demanded, his voice rising in a faint wail. "Dammit, you can't slip out like that. I didn't know where you went—"

"I was only going—"

"You've got to *tell me*!"

And for the first time since the copter went down, Mal heard something besides grim competence in Tevyn's voice.

He heard panic.

"Okay," he said, nodding. "Tell you. Got it—"

Tevyn shook his head. "No, man—you just disappeared, and you promised you'd stay."

Mal drew abreast of him. "I promised," he said again, but his heart was aching a little more now. "Trust me. I was getting firewood. Next time I'll tell you."

Tevyn nodded violently once. "Did you guys eat yet?"

"No. I was going to make a fire—"

"Good idea. I'll—"

"Tev?"

"Yeah?"

"I meant it. I won't leave unless you want me to."

"Then just don't," Tevyn said defiantly, and then he disappeared into their little shelter, leaving Mal to jump up and down on the set of branches until he had dried needles and twigs enough to set on fire.

**THE** fire made all the difference.

Besides Damien's lighter, there was a flint striker in the first aid kit and a little bag of cotton balls soaked in Vaseline tucked in a mint tin. Mallory had been nonplussed when Tevyn had first pulled that out, but then he'd put two of the cotton balls under a pile of dry needles and lit them on fire.

"Cotton's flammable," Mal said, eyes big as they caught a sturdy flame that quickly devoured the needles and then the twigs Tevyn was feeding it.

"It's also murder in the snow," Tevyn told him grimly. "Cotton kills. Don't take off that sweater."

Mallory had heard that saying before. The thing that made cotton great in the summer—its breathability, its ability to wick away moisture—made it a deadly way to lose body heat, especially when wet. The sweater Mal was wearing over his T-shirt and under his button-down was the most important layering piece on his body, but his wool suit coat came second.

A burst of wind came in through the remaining gap in the shelter, and Tevyn scowled at it. "We need to block that if we want to keep the fire, and I'm fresh out of fire blankets."

Mallory looked at Damien with apology in his eyes. "We could use my overcoat—but we need to find another pillow."

Tevyn stared at Damie thoughtfully, and his eyes went faraway. He went to his go bag and started rooting through it, pulling out things like plastic bags for wet clothes and a couple of sweatshirts, one of which looked surprisingly familiar, and a number of T-shirts, which he wore and replaced repeatedly as he sweat during activity. After mumbling something that sounded like "Goddammit, forgot the fucking rope!" he dumped the T-shirts into Damie's lap and then—carefully— swapped out the go bag for Mal's overcoat.

"C'mere and help me secure this," he ordered, and Mal didn't question him. The coat had cost nearly a thousand dollars, pure lamb's wool, with a thick satin lining. As he and Tevyn used the knife to poke holes in the corners and one of the lapels so they could secure the coat to the tree branch Tevyn had wedged against the cliff face and the other fire blanket, Mallory was very aware that his slick work clothes were the least of their worries.

"It's a nice piece," Tevyn said wistfully, surprising him. "I mean, you'll be able to wear it down the mountain—it should keep you warm and, to some extent, dry—but, you know, looked good on you."

Mal smiled a little, trying, and failing, not to be pleased. "Was hoping you'd notice," he said, working to lighten the mood.

"I always notice." Tevyn finished securing his end and waited for Mal to finish with his. Mal's fingers were warming now that they were out of the wind, and he hoped the fire would do even more.

He wanted badly to drag his knuckle across Tevyn's cheek, to do something tender, small, that would join them as human beings, remind them both that something had changed the night before.

But Tevyn whirled away, heading for the pile of gear he'd pulled out of the go bag. "Here!"

Mal caught his own CSU San Francisco sweatshirt in the face.

"You kept this?" Mal asked, pulling it over his suit jacket. He'd left the thing in the suite when he'd been part of the entourage for the Olympics. Tevyn had ended up getting X-rays, and Mal had needed to ask Harold to pack his suitcase for him so he and Tev could make it to the airport. That had been three years ago. He'd assumed it had ended up in a homeless bin in Aspen by now.

"It comes down to my knees," Tevyn said with a faint smile. "That over a pair of long johns is the best comfort wear in the universe."

But he avoided Mallory's eyes as he said it, and Mal's stomach warmed.

Tevyn hadn't even been in the suite—he'd been in the competitor's village, getting laid every night, from all accounts. But somehow he'd gotten hold of the sweatshirt, kept it close enough to be in his go bag with his pajamas, his comfort item.

Mal let him look away, but a completely nonphysical warmth took root in his stomach. The flush across Tevyn's cheeks, the way he was treating the sweatshirt like it was no big deal—he knew. Something really *had* changed the night before. Not something they could talk about now; they were trying to survive.

But if they could make it through the storm and get home, they would have something they needed to talk about.

They returned to the fire, which Damie had made bright and merry by feeding it from the pile of dry wood Mal had broken down and brought in, and Tevyn continued to be resourceful and clever.

The first aid kit he'd saved from the plane had an old-fashioned metal box inside the insulated nylon carry bag. Tevyn dumped the contents of the box—Band-Aids, antibiotic ointment, more gauze—and shoved them into a plastic Ziploc from his go bag. He set the carry bag aside, leaving Mal to wonder what plans he had for it, then scooped snow into the halves of the metal box. He set the box over some of the sturdier branches in the fire to melt the snow and pulled some high-protein broth packets from the go-bag pile and mixed them in the water as it melted. Then he funneled the mixture into one of the reusable bottles. They passed the bottle around, warmed and heartened by the food and the heat, and finally, Mal felt like he could think.

"Cell phones," he said. His had been tossed to the other side of the helicopter cabin before the crash. Getting it hadn't occurred to him.

"Bottom of the canyon," Tevyn said promptly.

"Mine too." Damien was still pale and in pain, but the painkillers and warm broth had done him a world of good. He huddled in his fire-blanket cocoon near their cheery little blaze and did his best impression of a slug on vacation, which was all Tevyn or Mal could ask of him.

"Well, that's good and bad," Tevyn told them, and they both nodded.

"Search party will show up to the base of the mountain as soon as the blizzard dies down," Damie said. "And guys, that's going to be three days, minimum. After that, they'll find the wreck, but they won't find us."

"Will they be able to tell where the wreck came from?" Mal asked, and Damie shook his head no.

"By the time rescuers get down there, it will look like I tried to land there instead of getting my ass flung on top of a mountain. If they *do* figure out where we landed, they'll still need to send people up here to find us."

"How long will that take?"

Tevyn and Damien both blew out a breath. "Anywhere from another three to fourteen days," Damien said, and then he and Tevyn came to some sort of agreement. "Or at least that's what my outfit would estimate," Damie added.

"Your outfit?" Tevyn wouldn't know this, but Mal had okayed Damien's time off and, in fact, had helped fund the venture.

"He works for a private search and rescue outfit," Mal said. "It's independent of government agencies, but they do work with the dog handlers in most areas."

Tevyn wrinkled his nose. Of course, profitizing a search and rescue operation had sounded like a bad idea to Mal, too, at first.

"So say there's a hurricane," Mal said, remembering Damien's friend's business plan. "And the government is doing all it can, but your daughter was going to school in the area and she's a hot mess about practical things."

"The Christie Newman case," Damien confirmed.

"You call Glen Echo's outfit, and they'll send a helicopter out for her and her friends. Once they get them to safety, they make themselves available to any agency that wants them—that's part of the caveat, that and cooperation—but they fly in and take care of that one person maybe nobody was looking for."

"But… but money…."

"There is a fee," Mal conceded. "But Glen's pretty good about taking stuff on account. In fact, probably better than most emergency rooms about not hounding a client until they can pay. And his prices are transparent online. He shows how much the overhead costs and how much profit he turns to keep things running. So far, people have been so grateful to have something they can do personally. People don't generally bail on the company that just saved their lives."

Tevyn grinned tiredly at Damien. "Look at you. Looks like a mild-mannered helicopter pilot, but you're really a sexy rescue worker. I'm impressed."

In spite of himself, Mal snorted, and Tevyn cast him a droll look.

"Would they count the blizzard?" Mal asked, not wanting to face how badly he needed to wrap Tevyn in his arms and never let him go. "I mean, toward days before they give up the search?"

"Yes," Damien said quietly. "Glen would give *us* some extra time because he's my friend and because we both did our stint in the Navy together and he knows I'm not going to do something stupid. So he'd look for us for a full two weeks—more if he found proof of life. But yeah. The three days nobody can look for us is going to count."

Tevyn sighed. "And making it up this mountain isn't going to be easy. The thing keeping us alive right now—the shelter—is the thing that'll keep us out of sight from a helicopter."

"So the question is, should we stay put after the storm?" Mal had read this once—one guy had built a shelter much like this one and burned everything he owned to stay alive. They at least had trees around them and fuel for their fire. Slogging through the snow was a risky proposition at best.

Mallory looked at Damie, whose pained grimace was everything.

"Damien?" Tev asked softly.

Damien gave a convulsive shiver, and Mal could see his features, pale and drawn—and starting to sweat. He gave Tevyn an apologetic smile. "I don't suppose you have any penicillin in your go bag?"

*Oh shit. Infection.* Mallory felt time beating at them as relentlessly as the snow.

"Not unless there's mold in the corners I don't know about," Tevyn said dryly. "How you feeling?"

"Do you want the 'I'm tough, I can do it' speech or the 'Feel like shit, do what you can' speech?"

"How about 'Feel like shit, but I can do it'?" Mal asked, hoping for a smile.

Damien swallowed and shivered. "It'll do for now."

But maybe not three days from now. Maybe not six days from now or ten. Mallory heard the subtext. Search and rescue might find them, but Damien might not last that long.

"Is there any way we can signal a helicopter after the blizzard?" Mal asked, thinking about the fuel they had. "The live trees have pitch. It's pretty flammable."

"That's an idea," Tevyn said, nodding. "Not that we want to try to burn the forest down either. Dead is dead whether it's fire or ice, you know?"

"Right." Mal sighed, suddenly exhausted. "Too bad we couldn't rig a sled of sorts for you. You could get down the hill in an hour and find search and rescue workers to lead them right to us."

To his surprise, Tevyn glared at him, blue eyes snapping with anger. "No! And don't even try that shit. I'm not leaving you two up here, and that's final."

"But you wouldn't be," Mal persisted. "You can get down there, find help—"

"And come back to a couple of people-sicles who died waiting for me?" Tevyn asked brutally, fury pulsing in every line of his body. "'Cause I saw that movie, and it sucked!"

"But, Tevyn," Mal said softly, "at least you'd be alive—"

"Without you? You said you'd stay. Was that bullshit?"

On the one hand, it was ridiculous. A promise to stay and comfort a grieving friend. Who took that to mean life and death in the middle of a frozen wasteland?

But Tevyn lived in a frozen wasteland—that was his natural habitat. That promise Mal had made, that all Tev had to do was ask, that was apparently bigger than they'd both realized that morning, warm and hurting in a safe hotel room.

That promise was coming down right now to whether Mallory stayed here and waited with Damien or hoped for the best and went down the mountain with Tevyn.

"No," Mal said, making sure Tev met him glare for glare. "I'm just saying, you know where my priorities are."

"Well, my priorities are none of us getting separated and none of us getting dead. We stay warm, we wait out the storm, and we start down the mountain when it's over."

"And we hope infection doesn't set in and I don't hit an artery and bleed out," Damien said, not backing down. "Because if either one of those things happen, you two need to ditch my—"

"Just shut up," Mal snapped. "We lost the argument, Damie. We all survive or none of us do. Deal with it."

"Finally talking sense," Tevyn muttered. His head and shoulders sagged then, infinitesimally, and Mal ached for him.

"Sst!" Damien hissed. Mal looked at him to see if something was wrong, and Damien rolled his eyes and then jerked his chin toward Tevyn, sitting alone on their little bench while Mal took the slope of the cliff face.

Mallory rolled his eyes, but his heart squeezed in his chest when he took in that sudden uncertainty, that struggle with grief and tension.

He stood up and stretched—which was probably a good thing, because his back was starting to chill being up against the stone—and then moved to the fallen tree to sit next to Tevyn.

Tevyn leaned his head against Mal's shoulder, and Mal wrapped his arm around Tev's waist. For a moment, that's all there was, the two of them, separated by layers of insulation, seeking closeness from the storm.

Tevyn shifted a little and shed his parka, then spread it out and laid it near the fire. He moved off the little bench to the ground and patted the parka next to him. Mallory sat, folding his legs, and was relieved when Tevyn leaned against him again.

"Maybe they'll find us as soon as the storm fades," Tevyn said after a moody silence.

"How much food do we have?" Mal asked.

Tevyn pointed to the go-bag pile. "We've got enough broth packets to last us five days, if we split two packets between the three of us, twice a day, and enough protein bars to last us four days, if we eat half of one every morning. It's not ideal—but it's not starvation rations either."

"Is there any way to warm the broth if we leave the shelter?" Because the prospect of warm soup was enough to make Mal think they could make it.

"We got hand warmers," Tevyn said, surprising him. "They last about four hours. We put one of them in that first aid carrying bag with the two reusable bottles of snow, we should have warm broth for lunch and dinner before we have to make shelter again. There's a box of 'em in there 'cause I'm a big whiny baby about warm hands before a run—"

Mal let out a small laugh. It was Tevyn's one diva moment as an athlete. His hands had to be warm. "Well, it just might save our lives."

Tevyn took off his gloves and grabbed Mal's hands. "Do you want one now?" he asked. His hands were so warm through the cashmere, Mal actually shivered.

"You're doing fine warming them up," he said, feeling foolish.

Tevyn gave a slow smile. "Yeah, Mal, I planned this whole helicopter crash special so I could make a move on you."

From across the fire, Damien gave a cross between a cough and a snort, and Mal tried to jerk his hands away.

Tevyn wouldn't let him. "I need to make sure they're warm."

"What about me?" Damien asked, sounding amused and cranky at once. "I have no gloves, remember?"

Tevyn's eyes widened comically. Damien's hands had been tucked inside the cocoon during their trek to the shelter, but he was right—his fingers were vulnerable, even in the warmth and safety they'd hastily erected.

"Oh yeah. Do you need one now?" Tevyn's willingness to please was amazingly charming.

Damien shook his head no. "My hands are pretty warm by the fire," he confessed. "I was… teasing."

He eyed the two of them speculatively, but Mal made no effort to move.

"He's warm," he said defensively.

"Yeah, Mal. That's it. He's warm."

Tevyn scooted closer, and silence fell in the little shelter. Exhaustion swamped Mallory, and a tiny corner of his brain started to catalog the aches and pains that had accumulated over the… morning?

"God. Tev. What time do you think it is?"

Tevyn yawned. "No idea." He grabbed one of the larger pieces of wood and put it on the fire, where it promised to burn for a while. "We can't let it go out," he told them. "Someone needs to add to that in an hour."

Mal thought about how much of the work Tevyn had done so far. "You sleep first," he said. "I'll wake you after I stoke the fire."

Tevyn yawned again. "Let me know if you're nodding off," he said, stretching out so his feet were near Damien's and his head was on Mal's lap.

Mal froze, suddenly as awake now as he had been exhausted thirty seconds ago. Tevyn relaxed into the bonelessness of sleep so quickly, Mal wondered if he

was injured. But then he remembered trips they'd taken
in the past, when Tevyn had kicked back in his seat,
pulled his sunglasses on over his eyes, and taken three
deep breaths. Boom! Out like a light.

Or the night before, when Mal had rubbed his back
as sobs racked his body, and then, in three deep breaths,
no sobs. Mal had gathered himself to stand, but Tevyn
had mumbled, "Stay. Please stay."

And once—just once—Mallory had given in to
the desire to hold him, thinking it could be mistaken
for friendship, for kindness, for the regard he'd always
held Tevyn as a client, as a friend.

Three deep breaths, and boom! Tevyn had fallen
asleep, but it wasn't until right now that Mal was
beginning to see the only mistake made the night before
had been by him—thinking he could hold that lithe
miracle of a body tight against his own and nothing
would change.

"He does that, the magic sleep thing," Damien
mumbled, shivering some more. The fire was going
pretty strong, the smoke siphoning up into a natural
chimney made by a thin spot in the pine branches
overhead. Cold, yes—but not freezing. Mal wasn't sure
if it was fever or shock, but he didn't like it.

"Should I get you some more clothes?" he asked,
and Damien shrugged.

"Anything there I could use as a scarf?"

Mallory rooted around under the sweatshirt Tevyn
had given him, which pulled tightly against his suit
jacket. He pulled off the flimsy cashmere scarf, heated
by his body, and threw it to Damien over the fire. Damie
caught it and wrapped it around his neck blissfully.

"Preheated. Thanks." He tried to grin, but then
his eyes fell on Tevyn, unmoving except for his steady

breaths. "But I wouldn't give me anything else of yours. He's liable to get the wrong impression."

Mal couldn't help it. He ran his hand along Tevyn's arm, stroking slowly. "We're not... I mean, we don't—"

Damien's sardonic snort was actually reassuring. "Don't love each other madly? Don't have sex yet? Don't think about each other that way? Pick your answer, Mal, but only one of them's not a lie."

Mal kept up that stroking, wishing they were somewhere warmer, somewhere Tevyn could feel his skin, somewhere not on top of this mountain, trapped in a blizzard, worried about their friend's life.

"We... he lets me take care of him," he said. Wasn't this wrong? Shouldn't Damien be helpless? But Mallory felt helpless about Tevyn, about touching him, about needing him. "He lets me take care of him now," he said quietly. "Have you seen what happens to his lovers?" Mal shivered. "I... I'd hate to be a hello in the hallway."

Damien grunted. "They weren't lovers," he said. "I've seen them too. They were... playmates. Kids playing around with their bodies. Why do you think he picked athletes? I don't think Tevyn's had a real lover in his whole life."

Mal remembered the moments he'd let fantasies slip into his consciousness, right before he fell asleep, when he was at his most vulnerable, his most afraid of being alone.

There hadn't been any playing around in those shadowy dreams—there had just been him and Tevyn and the way Mal's hands would shake as he cupped Tevyn's cheeks and held him still for a kiss.

"I'd be real," Mallory muttered, partly for his own reassurance. "It would be real." He made himself look up at Damien, to see if he was still awake. He was, feverish brown eyes looking at Mallory with more compassion than he could stand.

"Be brave, Mal. It might not break your heart."

Mal snorted and was abruptly too tired for emotion. He stared into the campfire, wondering what he could do to stay awake.

His mother used to hold pretend campouts in their backyard when he was a kid, gathering around a battery-powered lantern and pretending it was a campfire. He smiled and began singing.

"I'm an acorn, small and round, you can find me on the ground...."

Damien joined in on the chorus, and together they got through "I'm a Nut," "Ain't Gonna Rain No More," "Chicken Lips and Lizard Hips," and about thirty other campfire songs that they both remembered from what seemed to be happy childhoods. Damien eventually yawned and fell asleep, his shivering eased, and maybe his heart lifted.

Mallory hoped so.

He left Mallory holding Tevyn, who was still sound asleep. The fire had waned by then, and Mal put in the next log, gauging their firewood supply with a critical eye. It had felt like he'd gathered forever and ever and they'd have enough to last until spring. Looking now, he realized that somebody would have to venture out of the lean-to tomorrow and into the howling storm beyond. His overcoat gave a flap against its ties, and Mal stoked the fire carefully.

Tev knew more about first aid—it should probably be Mal.

Now that Damien was sleeping, Mal's campfire songs became melancholy. "Puff, The Magic Dragon" was followed by "Scarborough Fair," and then he had to lapse into musical theater. He'd finished off the soundtrack of *Les Mis* and *A Chorus Line*, half-mumbled under his breath before he caught himself nodding off.

*Come on, Mal. Just one more log. Let him sleep.*

Mal was frightened and alone. Night had fallen, and the wind howled around their flimsy shelter like a hungry, rabid animal, and the man he loved was asleep, vulnerable, allowing Mal to take care of him for the first time in his life.

He launched into *Something Rotten!* to give Tevyn another twenty minutes of peace.

# *Powder Keg*

**LIKE** Tevyn had suspected, the nonreusable water bottle turned out to have a use after all, one that all three men swore they wouldn't repeat to another soul.

It was just that Damien couldn't stand up and relieve himself outside like Tevyn and Mallory had—that crumpled piece of plastic was absurdly necessary.

But when that was done—thank God!—Mallory announced blithely that he was going to go into the storm and gather more firewood, and Tevyn wondered what would happen if he randomly punched the guy for being stupid.

"Have you even looked out there?" he snapped. "Have you *seen* what it's like outside of these three pieces of tinfoil and your overcoat? Because it's brutal,

Mallory. There's three feet of snow built up behind the lean-to. Did you see that?"

"I had to go out to pee just like you did," Mal snapped, and both of them shuddered. Now *that* was one piece of equipment nobody wanted exposed to the elements, but other than peeing on the rock wall—which had its own insulating layer of snow that had slid down from the night before—there was no choice.

"We'll do fine on the firewood we've got," Tevyn said stubbornly, but he knew that wasn't true. Mallory's even look told him he knew it too.

Tevyn pushed back the memory of Mallory curled up on his side, holding Tevyn against him so Tevyn could use his body like a throne to support his back. Tevyn had pulled his fingers through Mallory's straight black hair, admiring the decisive edge to his nose and the squareness of his jaw. He could recall vague snatches of singing from his own sleep, and once he was sure Mal was out, he'd sung all his grandmother's albums—John Denver; Gordon Lightfoot; Peter, Paul and Mary; Janis Joplin—so he could stay awake.

They'd kept him going until close to morning, when Damien had awakened and made use of the little bottle, and Tev had gotten a nap in while Damie warmed up the water for their morning broth.

Morning had felt like a surprisingly normal bit of camping then—a bunch of buddies in a tent, making do. It had been easy to pretend certain death wasn't battering at thin layers of fabric, trying to get in, and that they weren't going to have to subsist on scant rations and hope they found help before they ran out completely.

And Tevyn had been quite happy pretending that this was perfectly normal—that he could always spend the night with Mal's warm body next to him, that possessive hand splayed on his stomach or thigh, and that they could work around each other's grumpy, cranky morning bitchiness without coffee.

He'd been happy right up until Mal had mentioned the firewood, because the thought of Mal going out into the howling void was enough to stop his heart.

"Look," Mallory said, keeping his voice patient—a thing that made Tevyn want to throttle him, actually. "I get it. But you know how to care for Damien, and you know more about how to survive. I am expendable."

"That doesn't mean we should expend you!" Tevyn shouted, and to his surprise Mal got in his face—in that tiny little area—and shouted back.

"I don't plan on being expended! I just said we should think of something that will help me find my way back! Does that sound like I'm planning to walk into the snow never to return?"

"Like what? What are you supposed to use to find your way back? Even if I'd remembered my damned rope, should we tie it to your waist or something?"

Mal—and Damien, the damned traitor—both stopped as though thinking about it.

"Yeah," Damien said, coughing slightly. "Why not?"

Tevyn scowled. "Did you not hear me? What in the hell are we going to use for a rope?"

"I don't know." Mal stared fitfully at the pile of things Tevyn had pulled out of his bag. His eyes fell on one item in particular. "How many T-shirts do you pack in your go bag?"

*Oh Lord.* "Well, don't *I* feel stupid," he muttered. "I *was* saving them for bandages for Damien."

Damien blew out a breath. "There's one more actual dressing for today's change," he said, clearly dreading the process. "Then we'll need one for tomorrow, and one for the next day."

"So half a T-shirt for each day?" Mal hazarded. "What about after that?"

"After that we'll either be rescued or trying to get down the mountain." Tevyn swallowed. "Look, let me cut the shirts into ribbons. I can do it in one continuous strip. It might only take two, three T-shirts to get us enough rope so you have some room to go hunting. Don't worry about getting the dry stuff—there'll be lots of limbs knocked down. Grab what you can and haul it back—all of it. We'll stack it outside the door if it doesn't fit. Also, don't shy away from the long, skinny ones. We won't burn everything. I've got an idea to help us walk a little easier, if there's enough flexible branches."

An idea that sounded dumb and idealistic, but hell, they were going to be trapped in here for two more days anyway. It would give them something to do.

"So," Mal said, not like he'd won anything or with triumph, just matter-of-fact, like everything was going to be okay, "we change Damien's bandages first, then cut the T-shirts, and then I'll go get some wood."

*Well, hell.* "Yeah, fine. Here. Let's heat up some more water so we can clean the wound."

Tevyn moved around him so he could stick his body into the howling storm and scrape some pristine snow from the gap between the overcoat and the fire blanket—and get some space from the heated emotions inside the lean-to.

He came back and put the metal box up over the fire again, then started setting up everything he'd need. He gave Damien two ibuprofen tablets, which Damien washed down with his final mouthful of broth. And then he had a thought.

"Mal?"

"Yeah?"

"Remember when I hurt my wrist last year?" It had been a reactivation of his Olympic injury—painful, but not crippling.

"Yeah?"

"I just remembered I might have a few codeine tablets in my bag. If you can help Damie sit up and look through the zippered pockets...."

Mal found them while Tevyn was slicing a clean spiral cut around one of the T-shirts—one of his favorites, advertising Mal's company, and sky blue.

"Give them to him now with the ibuprofen," Tevyn said decisively. "We want him to be good and stoned when we open that bandage up."

Damie grunted, settling back down as Mal positioned the duffel bag. "Good friends," he said softly. He'd been quiet all morning, awake and lucid, but obviously consumed with pain. Tevyn missed his acerbic banter, but even more, he missed the buffer between himself and Mal.

Everything they wanted to say to each other, it had all been stifled these years by other people in the room. His trainer, his physical therapist, whoever he'd bedded the night before.

His grandmother.

The helicopter had spun through the air, and Tevyn's first thought—his only thought—had been Mal.

Not his grandmother.

Not his career.

Not his own life.

He'd wondered how they could die, Mallory Armstrong right across from him, and they'd never even kissed.

What was he doing wrong in his life that they'd never even kissed?

And here Mal—calm as a cucumber—was about to go into the howling storm to collect firewood because it was the most logical thing to do.

And they'd still not kissed.

Tevyn, who'd never claimed to be anything but king of the hill, wanted to claim Mallory, to kiss him, to make him so thoroughly Tevyn's that the storm wouldn't think about taking him.

Stupid.

So stupid.

Romantic in a way Tevyn had never known. Sex? Yes. Fantastic. Physical, fun, playful. Tevyn had friends all over the world—a good kiss with a hand down his pants was a perfect greeting.

But romance? Making someone "his"? Expecting a person to be there beyond the night? The event? The season?

Except... Mallory had been. For five years, Mallory had been there, and not even Tevyn's coach had been there that long. Gretta had replaced Turk Collins, who'd retired after Tevyn got his gold medal because, as he'd said, he was going out good and Tevyn couldn't give him a heart attack anymore.

Romance meant hearts, flowers, gifts, surprise visits—

Mallory showing up at three-quarters of his competitions when he didn't do that for his other clients.

Mallory risking a helicopter in a storm to tell Tevyn his grandmother was sick, and risking it again so Tevyn could visit before she died.

Mallory coming into his room because Tevyn had been crying—and staying because he was asked.

Maybe romance started with being a solid presence in a life that had become a merciless revolution of travel and the slopes. With being the guy who was there for everything, including sticking close to a scared kid in pain who had just won the Olympics and was wondering about life.

Maybe it was time for Tevyn to do something about romance and not leave Mal to do all the heavy lifting.

He finished spiral cutting the third T-shirt, leaving the other three for bandages and whatever else they'd need, and then tied the ends together before coiling the whole lot of it and setting it aside. He estimated around forty yards of rope there, all told. Given that they couldn't see five feet in front of them outside, that was more than enough.

"How you feeling, Damie?" he asked gently, and Damien gave him a loopy grin.

"This is as good as it's gonna get," he confirmed, eyes at half-mast. "It's gonna suck, but with any luck, I won't remember a damned thing."

Tevyn had set the T-shirt sleeves aside, and now he put them in the boiling water on the fire. Mallory took a deep breath and started unwrapping the person-burrito that Damien had spent the night as, stopping when they got to the blood-soaked pressure bandage around his leg.

"Four things we need to do," Tevyn said so they could get it out loud. "Need to strip the old gauze off, wash the wound, pack the wound with snow again, and wash the pressure bandage." The vinyl of the pressure bandage should be easy to sterilize with the boiling water, and so should the wound. "Then we can wrap the whole thing back again."

"Need to wash my hands first," Mallory said, his voice remarkably steady. "I'll strip the gauze and wash the leg. You wash the bandage and get the snow."

They exchanged a grim look and without another word got to work.

Damien, flying high on the codeine, was compliant and stupid, and Tevyn had to laugh to himself as he heard Mal being patient with him.

"Just lie back, Damien. That's it. Back. Lie back. Put your head back. That's it. Back. No, no, don't sit up. Don't sit—"

"Mother*fu*—"

"Yeah, it hurts. Just lie back. Let *me* deal with the leg."

"Leg doesn't work, Mal. Doesn't work. You're cute. But you're not Preston. Why aren't you Preston, Mal? I woke up this morning and wanted Preston. He won't even look at me if I'm not a Labrador retriever."

"Well, we'll have to get you back home so you can be a Labrador retriever for Preston! Okay?"

"Can't," Damien said glumly. "He's Gecko's little brother. No touchin' the little brother, Mal. That's a rule."

"Tell that to Blake Manning," Tevyn said, because Mallory was busy fishing out a strip of T-shirt from the water.

"Who's tha'?"

"Guy who plays for my favorite band," Tevyn told him, taking his own strip of T-shirt to wash the vinyl now that Mal had stripped the old gauze. They were working closely, head to head, and Tevyn suddenly wished he was clean. He wanted to smell like shampoo or cologne instead of fire smoke and sweat. "Three guys in the band are older brothers, and he just got engaged to the fourth, the baby brother. You gotta be honest about it, I think."

He'd seen interviews—the way Cheever Sanders had looked at Blake Manning had made him yearn for things he'd never voiced to himself before.

"He's young." Damien sighed. "Likes dogs more'n people. Don' blame him."

"That's hard when they're young," Mal said, eyes glued to his task. "You can want and want and want when they're younger, but you're afraid to make a move because what if you're taking something from them you can't give back."

Damien made a wordless howl then, because Mal was being thorough and relentless with the hot water, and then he went limp again, muttering to himself under the brain blanket of drugs.

Mal finished cleaning the wound, and Tevyn finished cleaning the vinyl in the sudden silence. Using pieces of T-shirt to guard his fingers, Tevyn took the pan of soiled water to the trench coat and stepped outside briefly to dump it on the rock wall, wipe it down, and fill it with fresh snow.

He was shivering hard when he got back in, and Mal took the container from his numb fingers and packed and rewrapped the wound without comment. He continued on by wrapping Damien back in layers of clothing Tevyn had used the day before, and finishing off with the fire blanket.

In the meantime, Tevyn had brought back more snow to melt. He handed Mal a wet clean T-shirt sleeve to wash his hands off on and then moved to his parka,

stretched on the ground to insulate his bottom, and
patted the spot next to him.

"Firewood," Mal said into the silence.

"Just rest here for a minute." They were both
sweating and shaking, because doctoring didn't come
easy to either of them.

"I had no idea he had a crush on Preston," Mal said
softly. "Sweet kid. Shitty with people."

"Good with dogs." Tevyn smiled slightly, because
they'd picked that much up.

"We have to get him home." Mal leaned against
him, giving Tevyn a little bit of his weight.

"All of us," Tevyn insisted.

"Okay."

"You're not stealing anything from me. I'm
twenty-five years old."

"Weren't when you walked into my office," Mal
said, voice softening. "You were nineteen and cocky
and had so many plans."

"And you helped me carry those out." He had.
Tevyn and Missy hadn't had much to offer back
then—but Mal had spun it into Tevyn's travel money,
his equipment, his supplies. Tevyn could jump on
a helicopter with a duffel bag that would keep three
men alive for a week because Mallory Armstrong had
worked overtime trying to keep Tevyn's little one-man
corporation afloat until sponsors started gluing names
to the back of his ass.

"So much promise," Mal mumbled. "Had to make
sure you got to do everything you dreamed about,
right?"

"I've been dreaming about you since the Olympics,
Mallory." Tevyn took a deep breath, because there, he'd
said it. "What are you going to do about that dream?"

Mallory's hand, clean now, dry, came up to stroke Tevyn's back. "I guess we'll have to see when we get back," he said.

"When."

"That's what I said."

"It's a promise. *When* we get back. That means we gotta get back."

Tevyn felt the kiss on the crown of his head. "Sure."

"No, not 'sure' like I'm delusional. Say it Mallory… there should be something between Mallory and Armstrong. What's your middle name, anyway?"

Mallory snorted and stood up. "I'm not telling."

Tevyn half laughed. "What in the hell?"

"No. Seriously. I would rather go out into that storm and collect firewood than tell you my middle name."

Tevyn stood up and watched in surprise, and Mallory pulled on his hat and then his gloves, which had dried by the fire. He'd taken off his suit jacket in the lean-to that morning and put the hooded sweatshirt on over his shirts and the sweater, as well as one of Tevyn's promotional scarves because he'd apparently given his cashmere one to Damien. Now he pulled the suit jacket on over his sweatshirt and grabbed the last set of T-shirt sleeves from the pile and shoved one in each boot before sliding them on.

And the whole time Tevyn sputtered at him, because… because….

"You've known my name from the very first. Tevyn Simmons Moore, because my father's name was Mark Simmons, but he left my mom when she was pregnant. That's… that's half my life there, in my middle name, and you're not going to tell me your middle name?"

"Hand me the rope," Mallory said, his lips twisted into what looked to be a playful little smile. Tevyn paused before giving him the coil, double-checking the knots and making sure none of it was going to break because it was too thin.

"Don't tug on it too much," Tevyn told him, taking an end and tying it to Mal's belt loop. He tugged experimentally. "Can you feel that?"

"Yeah."

"Will you when you're out in the snow?"

Mallory grimaced, and Tevyn undid the knot and slid his arms around Mallory's waist. They paused as he retied it, looping it around a belt loop to make sure it didn't slide off, and Tevyn skated his hands over Mal's clothing, wanting to touch his skin.

"You need to not stay out too long," Tevyn lectured. "Make trips. I'll stand by the entrance—just drop the wood in, and I'll stack it and sort it."

"You are really bossy," Mallory said, still teasing.

"I don't even know your middle name. How are you going to go out into the snow and I don't even know your middle name? That's insanity. How can I…?" Tevyn stared up at him, and his body finished that sentence when his mouth couldn't make the leap.

*How can you go out there when I haven't even kissed you yet?*

He reached up to cup Mal's neck and pulled him down for a kiss.

Mallory didn't even hesitate. Like he'd been praying for that kiss his entire life, he opened his mouth and tried to devour Tevyn whole.

In Tevyn's entire life, he'd never been kissed like that. Like every searing nerve ending, like every giant pulse of his heart might break through his skin and send him rocketing skyward. That kiss was higher than any trick Tevyn had pulled on a half-pipe, faster than any downhill slalom, more intense than any combo run. He gasped and pushed forward, wanting more, the adrenaline of finding a new high pounding through his bloodstream like surf.

Mallory gave back, cupping his waist, pulling him closer, both of them struggling to feel the other's heat through layers and layers of clothing, through worry, through fear.

Tevyn let out a gasp and pulled back, shaking, and Mallory rested their foreheads together. "I'll be back," he promised.

"You'd better. I don't even know your middle name."

Mallory kissed him again, hard and fast, enough for Tevyn to know he'd been taken and claimed, and then he was gone, leaving Tevyn to clutch a coil of rope and stand by the lean-to entrance, checking to make sure Damien didn't wake up.

**THEY** had no watches. They had no phones. The sun was obscured by clouds and trees and snow. They had no way of keeping track of time. As far as Tevyn was concerned, centuries passed, punctuated by a clatter and Mallory's heavy breathing as he dropped branches and wood through the opening left by the flapping bottom of the trench coat.

Tevyn had wrapped the rope end around his wrist after the whole length had played out, and he spent his time organizing the piles.

Since they didn't have an axe or a saw, a big stack of it would have to start burning at one end and then be pushed through the fire pit as it burned—after Tevyn skinned it with his knife.

Some of it had actually been knocked down several days before. It wasn't seasoned, per se, but, again, there was enough decent pulp that they could use it.

It was the stuff with the long branches that caught Tevyn's attention, because most of that was green and flexible.

That stuff he stripped the needles off of, putting them in a pile to use as insulation on the ground of their little shelter. Yeah, his coat would be covered with pitch, but they'd all be warmer for the layer of needles between them and the ground.

He spent the next century or millennium or whatever checking the rope on his wrist obsessively, making sure it indicated movement, indicated Mallory moving around to get firewood, indicated that he hadn't just keeled over in the storm and given up on life in general.

Finally, after he dropped the fourth load at the edge of the shelter, an exhausted Mal stumbled in, the slack from the rope trailing behind him.

"Sit," Tevyn ordered tersely. "There's the second ration of broth in the bottle. I'll take care of the rope."

He coiled it quickly, ignoring the chunks of Sierra snow and ice falling off of it by the entrance, and hung it over the fallen tree bench when he was done. They weren't finished with that by a long shot.

Then he organized and stacked the last batch of firewood and helped Mal off with his suit jacket and his hat, leaving the scarf on until the shudders stopped.

"H-h-h-hi, h-h-h-oney, I'm h-h-hommme," Mal gasped after a minute, and Tevyn smacked him on the top of his head.

"God, could you have been gone any longer?"

Mal looked at the piles Tevyn had set up and grimaced. "Th-that's not much wood for th-the effort," he managed, and Tevyn's next touch on his head was softer.

"It'll last us till tomorrow," he said. "If you help me strip the bark off the outside."

"Sure. Wh-why are we doing that again?"

Tevyn smiled. He'd grown up in a small cabin with a Franklin stove as a primary source of heat. "So it doesn't smoke and sputter," he said. "Outside's got most of the water in it, and the sap."

"Gotcha."

"It'll last us till tomorrow," he repeated. He thought about the estimates of how long the storm had to run its course. "You only have to do that one more time."

Mallory half laughed. "I'm not sorry about that." He wrapped his arms around his knees. "What are you doing there? With those long ones?"

"Well, I'm trying to weave them together. I know it sounds dumb, but—"

"Snowshoes," Mal said promptly. He pulled back to peel big chunks of snow off his suit pants. "Good. You finish those, and I can test them out tomorrow."

"Have to use some of your rope," Tevyn warned, and Mal shrugged.

"I stuck close to the rock face today. Tomorrow I can swing out a little. Seriously, if I don't have to sink every time I step—"

Tevyn frowned. "Speaking of, take off your pants."

Mallory sat straight up. "One kiss and—"

"No! The snow is melting, and they're soaking. I should have made you take them off immediately. Dammit—take them off, and I'll shake the snow off outside."

Mal did with gratifying quickness, and Tevyn took them from him and allowed his eyes to linger.

"What?" Mal asked, meeting Tevyn's look from under his lashes.

"You... your body's real fine," Tevyn said after a moment of drinking in pale skin and a scattering of black hair. Mallory's legs were well developed—Tevyn knew he did a lot of walking and biking back in the city, and he worked out as well. But more than that, they were naturally slender but not skinny. Solid. Muscular. Leading to a taut backside.

Tevyn had to break the silence that had fallen over them, because Mal's front side was starting to interest him too, and now was not the time. "Your ass is a little skinny, but it'll do."

He ventured out into the storm—grateful that between the lean-to and the rock face, they had a small foyer with a windbreak—and shook the snow off the sopping wool slacks.

In spite of the cold, the flush in his face, in his chest, in his groin, didn't fade.

## *Risk Assessment*

**"WHAT** is that, a dream catcher?"

Mal looked over his woven mat of twigs on his lap and tried to keep a straight face. Tevyn had come up with the idea of weaving snowshoes, and it had been a good one. But Tevyn was like the dog Mal's mom had loved before she died—in constant motion, twitching even in sleep. It was probably what made him such an outstanding athlete, having all of that kinetic energy bottled up in a disciplined body.

It did not, however, make for a lot of patience when dealing with fiddly things like sap-soaked twigs.

Mal, who dealt with facts and figures and spreadsheets and the infinitesimal difference between decimal points, was apparently a natural at it.

He remembered his mom's knitting and yarn craft supplies, stacked in the guest room of her house after he'd moved in after her death, and thought he might want to do something with those.

"This is fun," he said calmly, selecting another slender twig. "My mom used to knit and crochet. I should take it up." He sat cross-legged, a spare sweatshirt on his lap to keep him warm while his pants dried, and something about doing arts and crafts by the fire seemed cozy and domestic in spite of the reality battering at their shelter outside.

"Missy loves it," Tevyn said, his voice only shaking a little. "When I was a kid, she used to drag me to this... this yarn festival in Loveland. The yarn was pretty—a thousand different colors—and there were people who made stuffed toys, which I was all for. But they were just sitting, with their hands moving. Maybe I was too young. Couldn't sit."

"Maybe she could teach you now," Mallory said carefully. They didn't know. Missy could have a month. Or she could have already passed. "Or maybe, we could... I don't know. Learn together."

Tevyn gazed at him, lips parted in what was apparently wonder. "Knitting?"

Mal's cheeks heated. "We do a lot of traveling," he said with a shrug. "To cold places. I mean, if I had my mom's knit bag, I'd be making us full-body sweaters right now."

"What... what was she like?" Tevyn asked.

Well, of course. Mallory had needed to get personal with Tevyn and Missy. He'd needed to know their finances, and there were few things as personal as that. But Mal—he'd needed to be dependable. You didn't get to talk about your mother when you were dependable.

But neither of them had anywhere to go, and talking about his mother, whom he had loved, was so much better than telling Tevyn he was scared.

"She was amazing," Mallory said softly. "She started dyeing her hair as soon as she went gray. Not brown or blonde, but pink and purple, long before it was fashionable. She would do regular mom stuff— bring home sugar cookies in the tube after work and then cook them and let me decorate. Cook spaghetti for my birthday. But we didn't have a lot of money. My dad died when I was little, and she was single and working. And she'd find… just things to do. There was always a park to walk to or a sunset to see. She would make up these really… enchanting games, and sing songs. I… love musical theater. Not because *I* love it but because she used to sing all the words to *A Chorus Line* and we'd act it out in the living room. When I started my business, the first thing I did was get season tickets at the Orpheum and took her to every show."

Tevyn had stopped working on his snowshoe and was looking at Mallory with ginormous, luminous eyes. "Did she like that?" he asked.

"Oh yeah. She—even after she got sick. She would put on a wig and her best dress, and we would go see *Wicked* or *Newsies*. I think she was trying to hold on for *Hamilton*, but…." He couldn't finish that sentence. "She just really loved it. I'm… I don't seem to have that sort of poetry, you know? I… I guess we were always so hurting for money. I wanted to make sure people who needed it could find a way to do the things they wanted. It's what I wanted for her."

Tevyn swallowed, his Adam's apple bobbing. "She sounds… wonderful. When did she pass?"

"About a year before you walked into my office." Mal shrugged. "We'd only recently located there, you know. Had been on the ground floor out in Burlingame—took us four years to make enough money to have an office up in the sky."

"Did she get to see that?"

"No. But she wouldn't have cared. The fact that I'm single—*that* she would have cared about."

Tevyn let out a half laugh. "Did she care about you... you know...?"

"Being gay? No. I mean, she'd been an actress in college. I think half her friends were gay."

Tevyn shrugged. "I... I guess I was just crazy about sex. Boys, girls—it was like there was always a new trick to learn, you know?"

Mal snorted softly. "No. I mean...." He bit his lip, thinking about that kiss. That amazing, sensitizing kiss that had revved his battery, kept him warm during his interminable trek for firewood. "I've always sort of suspected it would be a lot of fun, but you know...."

Tevyn was staring at him.

"What?"

"You've had relationships!"

"Yes! Five!" Mal swallowed and wondered, if they were going to die up here in this arctic wasteland, why he couldn't have gone *before* he'd said that, and *after* that epic kiss. "Uhm, several," he amended.

Tevyn was regarding him with the openmouthed fascination of a cat who could taste prey on its palate.

"Five, you say?"

"It's not, a... you know, plethora."

Tevyn smirked. "A plethora. No. No, it is not. So tell me about this five. I'm *dying* to hear."

"I'll tell you my middle name instead!"

Tevyn shook his head. "Oh, no. I'll *guess* your middle name, Mallory Andrew Armstrong—"

"Nope."

"Either way, I'll guess it. But *this*, you have to tell me."

"Why?" The snowshoe in Mal's hand was almost forgotten, until Mal realized if he wove it a little tighter, he wouldn't have to see Tevyn's predatory gleam. "Why is it so necessary? You notice *I* don't ask you names—"

"Because that would cover the athletic roster of the entire circuit," Tevyn said dismissively, "including girlfriends, boyfriends, trainers, and a couple of physical therapists younger and hotter than Harold. If you're fooling around with everybody, you're not serious about anybody. Not one of those people lasted more than two nights, tops. But *you*—you've been auditioning for happy ever after, and I'd like to know the competition."

"One of them's a girl," Mal said, arching an eyebrow playfully, like maybe that would stop this madness. "You really want to hear?"

"God, it's like somebody wrote a soap opera just for me! Now shoot!"

Augh!

"So, Chris—"

"The girl?"

"No, my high school boyfriend. Closet case. Said he loved me, hearts, flowers, the works, then told his family Mallory was a girl's name."

"Asshole," Tevyn snapped.

"Deeply afraid," Mal corrected with compassion. "He's come out since. Wasn't pretty. You and I got lucky. I try not to forget that."

"You're a really good person. Now spill. First base, second base, third base, twins and a trapeze in the homestretch?"

"Some necking," Mal told him, smiling in spite of himself. Tevyn's practicality made the pain of adolescence seem exactly that—adolescent. Almost nostalgic. Like Tevyn could laugh at those things in himself too. "Once, there was a mutual hand job that has gone down in my hall of fame."

Tevyn grunted. "So *not* the one that got away."

"No."

"Go on."

Mal had to laugh. "Courtney."

"The girl?"

"Nope. College boyfriend. Was headed somewhere back East after college. We had an amicable split."

"Did you have amicable sex, Mal? Because even if this guy took your cherry, I'm not feeling it."

"I took his," Mal told him, face burning. "It was pleasant on both sides."

Tevyn's sputtering laugh told him everything he wanted to know about "pleasant" sex, and it wasn't flattering.

"So two swings and two whiffs. Did you try the girl for shits and giggles, you know, to see if you got it wrong the first time?"

"My middle name could be Hungarian, you know. My mother's family was Hungarian. Maybe it's Slyzyk."

"I don't even know what that was you just said, but I know that's not your name. I got close, didn't I? That's why you switched subjects. Did I guess right about the girl?"

The hell of it was, he had.

"Her name was—"

"Lucinda?" Tevyn hazarded, and Mal grinned with all his teeth.

"Charlie."

"*No!*"

"I shit you not."

"Your business partner?"

*God. So embarrassing.* "The very same."

"But she doesn't even like me!" Tevyn's horror was comical.

Mal grimaced. "That's not true. She just… you know."

"No, I don't." Tevyn was looking at him like this was serious, and Mal blew out a breath, remembering all the times Charlie had greeted Tevyn with short words and narrowed eyes.

"She's not stupid, Tevyn. She knew I was… not rational about you. She worries. She was there when I lost my mother, and there when I broke up with Keith. She uh, doesn't trust someone who might hurt me."

"Well, tell her I won't. I want to like her. But you slept together? Because that changes everything!"

"You should still try to like her," Mal said, hoping he hadn't ruined everything with this little secret. "Because it was a terrible mistake. It's just…." *How to explain this?* "You know—we had so much fun setting the business up, and we got along so well, and it seemed like it would be so…." Oh, this didn't reflect well on him.

"Easy?"

Mal sighed. "Yeah. But I was watching extreme amounts of porn to make her not feel bad whenever we had a date. About four weeks in, we met at a restaurant, and she ordered a bottle of wine for each of us and said,

'We're toasting our friendship, Mal. And our business. Because that other thing is *so* not us.'"

Tevyn let out a sigh. "Man, I can't even make fun of that. That's… so grown-up."

"Yeah. Yeah, it was. So my next relationship was not."

"Really?"

Mal's cheeks burned. "A porn model named Skylar. Great kid. Came down to a dance club, right after me and Charlie called it quits. I was pounding vodka. I woke up naked, and he said I'd hit high C."

Tevyn did one of those things where you're trying not to laugh so you choke on your tongue. "Did you?"

Mal hid his face behind the screen of branches he was weaving. "I have no idea. I've never been so drunk in my life."

"So did you date?"

"God no. I kissed his cheek, took two ibuprofen, and fixed him breakfast, and he kissed my cheek and told me he had to be in Sacramento for class the next day."

"And you called that a relationship?"

Mal's mortification was complete. "It was supposedly the best sex I've ever had. I figured he should get mention."

"Kaden," Tevyn ventured.

"No."

"Richard."

"No."

"Dallas, Texas, Austin, Dalton, Tyler, Taylor, or Madison."

"No."

Tevyn's voice dropped, all teasing gone now. "Then tell me about Keith."

Mal sucked in a breath. "Keith was… well, he was supposed to be it. The real thing. Not an audition. He was a probate lawyer. We'd used his firm in the past. He was steady and kind. Had a cat, a dog, a small house on the peninsula. Rode BART in on the commute. Liked the theater. We'd go up to the foothills or to the beach on our weekends off and go hiking or see a show. Like you see people do in movies or hear about on TV. We made plans for the future and everything. I thought, you know, by the end of the year, we'd move in together."

"What happened?" Tevyn asked, but he was looking at Mal like he knew.

"The Olympics," Mallory told him. "And suddenly that time we'd spend antiquing or walking on the beach, I was spending in a helicopter, on my way to God knows where, watching you fly down a hill."

Tevyn swallowed, and his eyes grew bright. "Do you want me to say I'm sorry, Mallory Seymour Armstrong?"

"No—and no." Mal looked away. "I want you to know... this thing you're doing, where you're telling me we need to bare our souls to each other, and you're asking me about my past lovers, and you're looking at me like... like lunch—"

"Way, way better than lunch. Dinner at least," Tevyn said soberly—which, considering how hungry they were, was a serious thing.

"Like Wagyu Kobe beef and lobster," Mal amended breathlessly. "This is important to me. This... I will do anything you want, Tevyn. I will stay away and let you live your life. I will... will move to Colorado, business and all. I will give up all my clients and follow you from place to place like a bird on the wing. But you need to know I gave up... a relationship, a good one, just to see you fly down a snowy hill and do impossible things in the air."

Tevyn set his mangled mess of weaving down by the fire and moved to hands and knees, until he was right in front of Mallory.

Very carefully he pushed on Mallory's wrist until Mal set his own weaving aside, and the only thing in their little cave, with the cheery fire beside them and the howling wind outside, was Tevyn's sober blue eyes.

"You lied," Tevyn whispered.

"I did not. My middle name's not Seymour."

Tevyn shook his head slowly. "You lied about not having poetry. All those people I'm not naming? Not a soul has said anything to me as important as that."

Mal closed his eyes, expecting the kiss, and he was not disappointed.

Tevyn's mouth was soft, warm, and proprietary, and Mal's heart started hammering in his ears louder than the storm. Tevyn didn't move from his hands and knees, and Mal would have to disentangle his legs to do more, but the kiss simply blazed up between them, hot, hotter, explosive, with nowhere else to go and no more tinder to burn. It blew up—lips, tongues, teeth, no exploring, simple sensual annihilation.

Mal groaned, lifting his hands to Tevyn's cheeks to hold him in place, to plunder more, and Tevyn pushed forward instead until Mal was on his back, Tevyn on top of him, his bare legs wrapped around Tev's hips as they necked breathlessly on the ground.

The fire popped next to them, and Tevyn startled, scooting off and looking around wildly.

Mal couldn't even laugh. "Fire," he muttered.

"Dammit." Tevyn rocked back onto his knees. "Dammit, we're not doing this here."

"Thank God," Damien mumbled. "'Cause that would have been awkward."

Mal threw his arm over his eyes in mortification. "Don't suppose we can all pretend Damien was too stoned to see that?"

"Since I thought he was asleep, that's an awesome idea," Tevyn muttered sourly.

"Maybe I could just die and save you the embarrassment." He didn't sound like he was joking. *Why wasn't he joking?*

Tevyn and Mal shared a look of panic and then looked back to Damien, who *had* been sleeping peacefully.

His face was paler than it had been after the bandage change, and his cheeks were flushed when the little shelter was still chilly, but not deadly cold.

"Need another ibuprofen?" Tevyn asked, voice clinical, as though they hadn't been busted necking on the ground like schoolkids.

"Would be grateful. Have we had our protein bar yet? My stomach's not happy with all the meds."

"Not yet," Tevyn said. "Mal, you keep weaving like the expert you are. I'll do everything else."

"Bossy," Damien muttered. "He's bossy."

"Incredibly," Mallory agreed, focusing on his tightly bound mat of branches. "So, uh, how much did you—"

"I faded out when he asked about your sexual history, which means you have *got* to step up your game."

Mal let out an embarrassed chuckle. "I'll let you know if that changes."

"You will not," Tevyn snapped. "That's gonna be between you and me. He doesn't need to know a damned thing."

Mal stared at him as he busied himself around the shelter, the line drawn between his blond eyebrows stating he clearly meant business.

"Uh…."

Tevyn's look at him was… lazy. Lazy and leonine. "You won't need to tell everyone, Mal. They'll know."

"Uh…."

"Yeah," Damien added, taking the ibuprofen tablets from Tevyn gratefully. "But will they know Mal's middle name? Is that game still going on, or did Tev figure it out when I dozed off?"

"Nope," Mal said, letting a small smile of triumph twist his mouth as he worked.

"George," Damien hazarded.

"Nope."

"Grover," Tevyn tried.

"Nope."

"Kendall," Tevyn tried again.

"Nope—but that's a nice name!"

"It is," he agreed. "You seem to go for unisex, and I thought it would fit."

"In my exes, not myself!"

"Fair enough—*Mallory*." Damien took the flask of melted water from Tevyn and swallowed. "Percival."

"Nope."

"Gerald," Tevyn tried.

"Nope."

"Carlton."

*Nope, nope, nope*—but at this point, Mallory wasn't sure if he'd answer yes if they stumbled upon the right name by accident.

The game was keeping them occupied and happy and not freaking out about the storm, and it was letting him weave his tight little mats that would hopefully be enough to walk on top of the snow.

And it was letting Mal not dwell on the things he and Tevyn had said with only the fire and the snow as witness, things he was almost afraid to admit he'd said.

Tevyn had damned well better be serious about the two of them, whatever his idea of an endgame was. So far he'd stripped Mal naked and dissected his heart with almost a clinical precision.

If this was all worry over Grandma Missy and being alone, or fear because they were trapped in a storm and might not make it home, Mal might not ever leave this place in his heart, naked and alone in front of a survival fire, unable to protect himself from Tevyn's most outrageous whim.

Not wanting to protect himself.

Wanting Tevyn's attention on his heart, his soul, more than he'd wanted dignity, or safety, in his entire life of making them his quest.


**WHEN** they'd first started their business, Charlie had told Mal she wanted to be like Rapunzel in the movie *Tangled*, without the weird hair. She wanted to be a dream pusher, and Mal felt the same way.

But neither of them were stupid, and they weren't stupid about themselves either.

Whenever clients came into Mallory's office, asking for help to start their companies, start their dreams, or invest what they were making to make their dreams bigger, Mallory and Charlie would do a risk assessment.

It was common practice with any investment firm, but Mal and Charlie always added a twist.

If Mal really liked a client, he'd give the numbers to Charlie, and vice versa. Without meeting the client, the other one would assess them, just based on paper.

And then they'd sit down—usually at dinner, once every two weeks, because they liked each other's company—and talk.

"Charlie, they've tanked four other businesses before this one. Lingerie is selling online more and more these days. Have you checked out other businesses similar to it, the ones with a store front? Those businesses are tanking too. Maybe advise they do online to start."

"Mal, you're trying to back an adult film company—"

"I'm trying to back an adult film company that wants to hire its actors *out* of porn. Look at this business plan, Charlie. I haven't seen anything this airtight since new Tupperware."

"Charlie, go for it. I know the numbers are touch and go, but look at what they started with. If they can get this much capital with the sweat off their backs and their street smarts, imagine what they can do with your TLC."

"Mal, Mal—you got a soft heart. I'm telling you, those numbers are marginal. He's what? A snowboarder? Is that even a real goddamned sport?"

"Yeah, Charlie, it's a real sport. And you should see them. This grandmother? She sold off a ten-acre lot of her property to invest in her grandson. And her grandson would snowboard off a cliff if he could wave to her while he did it. Every commentator on the circuit says he's going to be the next big thing. Just a little more exposure and he'll have sponsors knocking at his door. All he needs is the money to get in there and win."

Mal had won that one. He didn't always. He had taken a few hits, yes, but so had Charlie.

Their gains had been bigger than their losses. And more importantly, their consciences were clear.

Over the next twenty-four hours, Mallory ran a risk assessment in his head maybe thirty times an hour.

He'd weigh the odds of somebody coming for them in their snug little shelter with dwindling rations but enough heat to live.

He'd weigh them against going out into the forest and trying to get down the mountain.

He'd weigh them against getting lost or falling into a hole in the snow—he knew those happened, particularly in icy conditions like this, where the glaze on the top didn't necessarily equal stability underneath.

He'd take those odds of somebody looking at the wreck of the helicopter, not finding any bodies, and making the leap to the peak above them and pit them against starvation, injury, wild animal attack, and death from exposure.

And then he'd look at Tevyn, face grim, as they both watched Damien grow more taciturn, quiet, and feverish, and weigh those odds against their friend's life.

And against the ever-increasing weight of hope that Tevyn seemed to rest squarely in Mallory's lap.

"We can make it," Tevyn would say with confidence. "You, me, Damien—we keep him in a travois, and we can get him down that hill. Right, Mal?"

And Mal, with his risk assessment brain, would shut down right there. Would stop assessing. Because Tevyn had heard the odds of his grandmother getting up and leaving her hospital bed—and they were nonexistent.

The odds of the three of them making it down the mountain alive were marginally better.

And Mallory couldn't—*couldn't*—be the person who told him that it was a damned slim margin and they'd be better off letting Damien die while they watched and then ate his food.

In his head, he heard Charlie. "I don't know, Mal—not a great bet. I mean, you work out, sure, but you're gonna carry a whole other human? This isn't an urban street, Mallory. I'd give you even odds at least, strolling down the business district, especially in your pinstripe."

And in his head, he replied: "Charlie, I've bet so much of myself on him already. What's my life? Seriously? Could I live with myself if I didn't take this one? I'm thinking no. I'm thinking I may have to take the hit."

And that's when he'd look at Tevyn over the snowshoe he was weaving—that was his job now as Tevyn and an increasingly delirious Damien tried to guess his middle name, how many pets he'd had as a child (five), and what was his favorite color (the color of Tevyn's eyes—he was holding out for "porcelain blue").

"Yeah," he'd say, like there wasn't any other answer. "You and me can do this. We've got supplies. We can build another fire. Let's wait until the storm dies down and get our bearings. Then we can figure out our next move."

That's what he'd say.

And then he'd pray to his mother and any listening saint that somehow search and rescue would find them, on top of a random mountain, underneath a random tree.

# *Real Risk*

**MALLORY** started slurring his words, fumbling his tongue, twitching as he worked, and Tevyn realized he was exhausted.

However long he'd been out looking for firewood, it had tuckered him out, and even as he fielded questions—*Dermott? Calvin? Calvin would be good. We could call you Mal-Cal! Did you have a dog? A cat? A goldfish? One at a time? Wait, a pet rat? Those are good! Oh! I've got it! Chartreuse!*—his hands stilled on the second snowshoe.

Tevyn, who had been peeling the bark off the biggest of the green branches to make them easier to burn, put down his project and tugged gently at the tightly woven mat of twigs in Mal's hand.

"We have all tomorrow," he said softly. "You sleep first tonight."

Mallory yawned and slumped a little sideways. Tevyn moved the prepared wood to the pile he and Damien could both reach, then folded his knife and slid it into his pocket.

"I can stay up," Mal claimed, hand over his mouth. "I mean, it can't be that long after dark, can it?"

"I don't know, Mal. I know you've got bags under your eyes, and you've been keeping us occupied for hours. It's time to sleep."

Mal grunted. "I hate to leave you alone," he said plaintively. "How's Damien?"

"Asleep." In the time it had taken for Mal to stop weaving. "He's… he's feverish." Tevyn had made him drink melted snow every so often, using it as an excuse to feel his forehead. Damien had been burning up the last time, and the ibuprofen would only last a couple more days.

Mal scrubbed at his face, and Tevyn set one of their bigger logs on the fire, then poked at it until he was sure it would burn. Their fire pit was becoming a pronounced thing, a ring of ashes surrounding the flames on the bare ground. The heat from the fire and the heat from the three humans in the little shelter—as well as being under the spread of the pine trees and next to the rock face—had pushed out against the snow, until there was none on the ground around them. The building snow from the blizzard pushed against the fire blankets on three sides, creating a more-than-snug little cocoon, and it was tempting—so tempting—just to concede to common sense and stay there until they were found.

They could live for five days on water alone. Five days would be enough, wouldn't it?

But Damien's wound hadn't looked good—and it wasn't going to get better on its own. Leaving Damien here alone felt like a death sentence. Leaving without Mal was unthinkable.

"Here," Tevyn said, stretching out with his back against the shelter wall and his front to the fire. "We have enough wood for the night. Lie down in front of me."

Mal didn't question him, which was fine, because the truth was, they were doing this purely because Tevyn wanted to touch Mallory Armstrong's body.

They situated themselves, and Tevyn slid his bare hand under Mal's shirts, feeling the satin softness of his tight stomach and the silky hairs of his happy trail. Mal gasped.

"Cold?" Tevyn asked.

"Little. Feels good."

"Yeah. I like being touched." Tevyn chuckled. "But then, you could probably figure that out."

"This feels more personal than that," Mal admitted sleepily.

"Probably because it is." Tevyn ventured a little higher, finding his chest and squeezing gently. "Not gonna go at it like bunnies. I just want to learn your skin."

Mal hummed. "My skin is grateful," he said, and Tevyn laughed. Mallory was funny. It was something he'd known in a peripheral way. Small one-liners, the dry way he had of delivering news. But the way he bounced his words off Tevyn's, responded smartly to Damien, kept the banter going in the shelter—all of that told Tevyn that he was probably dry and funny as a rule, not an exception.

"I'm the one who's grateful," he said, burying his face against the back of Mal's neck. "I mean, I could have been stranded with someone who wanted to bang me for three days but didn't care what my name was."

Mal snorted. "I go to your competitions just to hear them say your name. 'Tevyn Moore, coming down the slope, a full second ahead of the leader in this heat!' and everybody loses their mind. 'Tevyn Moore, executing a laid-out 720 with a twist—folks, that's the only time you'll see that trick at this competition, and Moore is the only one who'll be doing it.'"

Tevyn laughed and rubbed his cheek against the five layers of clothes between him and Mal's back. "I never hear the announcer," he confessed. "I hear the crowd roar, but never the announcer."

"That's part of why I started backing athletes," Mal told him. "It was such an awesome thing—and then we could hear the crowd roar, and I'd see you do something amazing, and...."

"And what?"

"And... and I'd helped that really talented person do that really awesome thing. In a small way, you know? And you—Charlie didn't even think it was a real sport. But my mom and I used to watch the Olympics. First time I heard Linkin Park, I was watching Shaun White win a gold. I... you walked into my office, and I so wanted to see you fly."

"You were so smart," Tevyn told him, feeling small. "And so cool. And you just laid it out, how you were going to fund our equipment and how some of the sponsor money would pay you back and the rest would be reinvested. I've got a high school education, Mallory. I walked out of your office thinking that someday I wanted to be as smart as you were, so you and me could...." Oh, it was hard to say.

"What?"

"Like the other night. So I could walk into a bar and say something to make you smile, and you and me would dance."

"What now?" Mal asked. "Now that we've danced."

"I'd only really be stupid if I let you get away."

Across from them, Damien let out a whimper, and they were both grimly quiet.

"He needs to be okay," Tevyn said at last. They couldn't go home and be happy if they knew it had cost them their friend.

"He needs to tell Preston he loves him."

Tevyn thought about that. "Do you think he will?"

"God, Tevyn, I don't know. You and I have been stupid for nearly five years. The human heart has an IQ of twelve."

Tevyn let out a chuff of breath, but he didn't say the obvious thing, the thing weighing on his heart and his mind.

He did hold Mallory tighter, though, so tight, maybe his heart, his spirit, his mind, his body, would all stay right here in his arms where they belonged.


"TEV, wake up!" Mal shook his arm roughly, his voice rising. "Baby, we need to dress Damien's leg—stat!"

Tevyn grunted. He'd stayed awake as long as possible the night before, replenishing the wood two more times after Mal had dropped off. Mal had taken over for the early morning shift, and Tevyn was surprised to be awakened so soon.

"We have to what?"

"Look at him!"

Tevyn sat up groggily and frowned. Damien was sheet-white, feverish, and shaking, not particularly conscious at all.

Oh yeah. They needed to change that dressing. They could probably pour boiling water on that leg and not do any more damage than what was going on inside it right now.

"We need a poultice," he muttered. "Something hot to draw the heat out."

Mal grunted and looked at the strips of drying washrags hanging around the shelter. "I think we need to boil a lot of frickin' water."

Again and again they brought the battered little metal box of water to a full boil, sterilizing bandages and washcloths or heating strips of T-shirts to lay across Damien's wound. Tevyn raided his go bag and came out with his shaving kit and some antibacterial soap that he used to soak bandages in, and he prayed that helped. They'd set a water bottle up on a hand warmer to defrost their drinking water, and Mal—Mal went out three different times, into the howling wind, to come back with more firewood.

Tevyn wasn't sure what finally tipped the scales. Maybe it was when he lost patience and dumped half a box of scalding water on top of the pad of T-shirts on the swollen, oozing wound.

But suddenly Damien gave a cry, and the wound itself welled up with yellow-white fluid that burst out of the bandages and ran down Damien's swollen, blackening leg. Tevyn gave a little whimper and started cleaning things up, the smell of infection almost overwhelming.

Mal was outside, collecting the final round of firewood for the day, and Tevyn looked at the rope tied around his wrist and realized that it was limp—had been, in fact, since right before Damien's wound had begun to seep.

"Oh crap." Tevyn hurried up and cleaned, piling the used bandages in a corner near the snow, not sure if they had it in them to be boiled one more time. He left Damien's wound open, covered lightly with gauze, and grabbed the metal box, thinking he could call for Mal while he was filling it up.

Mal had needed to dig his way up through the fresh layer of snow to leave the shelter that morning. Tevyn had to follow the same path up to get far enough to safely dump the contaminated water and wipe down the box with melted snow and dry it out with one last clean scrap of T-shirt. The tunnel floor was getting tamped down—it was easier this time—but the snow kept coming. He spent some time looking around, squinting against the snow and shivering and saw nothing. And the rope around his wrist remained limp. *Hell.* He ran back into the shelter and set up the water to warm, put on his parka and his gloves, and ran back up to the top, pulling the slack of the rope back as he did so.

And calling Mal's name.

The rope caught on something—something heavy, and Tevyn pulled on it as hard as he dared. Nothing— he couldn't even see trees in that direction.

Frantically he looked around and could see only the sapling he'd used to secure Mal's trench coat.

He unhooked the rope from his wrist just long enough to wrap it around the sapling, pulling the extra coils with it before securing it back on his wrist. Mal had said yesterday that he'd used up all the wood by the rock wall, so Tevyn went in the other direction, playing out his T-shirt rope as he went, following the other rope in the snow.

If they hadn't been tethered together that way, if he hadn't been following fifty feet of T-shirt rope, Tevyn would have missed him.

Mallory had apparently stumbled into a hole—six feet, maybe—and was midway to covered with snow when Tevyn almost fell down the same goddamned hole.

"Mal!" he screamed, tugging at the rope. "Mal! Goddammit, Mal! Get up!" He wanted to jump in there and shake him, but he wasn't sure Mal could get out without someone to help him from the top side. Besides, they were both out of rope. Any more movement on their parts and they wouldn't be able to find their way back. Tevyn couldn't even see the glow of their campfire through the shelter walls from this far out.

"*Mal!*"

A faint groan reached his ears, and the lump on the ground started to struggle.

"Mallory Ambrose Armstrong, you get your ass up and you climb up here and get back to the fire with me! Goddammit! You promised!"

The figure struggled to his feet—and was still thigh-deep in snow. *Shit.*

"Mal! Mal, you've got to climb up here! C'mon, man! I can't dig you out from here. You've got to climb!"

Another groan, and Tevyn about lost his damned mind.

"*Mallory Armstrong, you don't quit on me, do you hear me! You promised! One other person on this planet ever promised me like that, and she's dying! You're not frickin' dying—stand up and get moving, you hear me!*"

"Yeah, Tev. Don't panic. Sorry. Took a spill." He was barely loud enough to be heard over the wind, but Tevyn wanted to laugh and cry at the same time.

"Took a spill? You think that's all? You fell in a frickin' hole! Now you feel me tugging?"

"Yeah. Why you doing that?"

"'Cause I've found the lower lip of the hole. Follow me!"

Tev went until his rope pulled taut enough to break. "Now climb!"

Mallory nodded, and one hand, one foot at a time, began to climb groggily to where Tevyn practically danced, waiting for him.

The dancing helped. He was packing down the snow, stomping a path for Mal to get to eventually, and even though it was icy, it was better than falling through.

Finally, *finally*, Mal was close enough for Tevyn to offer his hand and pull him up, one step at a time, toward the shelter.

"I didn't get firewood!" Mal yelled when it became clear they were following the two ropes back.

"I don't care!" Tevyn shouted in return. "We've got enough!" Hopefully. They might have to burn the bark he'd peeled off, but the stuff from the day before might be drier. Hell, they had scraps of soiled T-shirt to burn, old gauze, Tevyn's pitiful attempts to make snowshoes from the day before.

Mallory's had been better. They'd been going to try out his little shoes today, but Damien hadn't woken up, and they didn't have time.

They'd even burn those if they had to. Burn the go bag, burn Mallory's wrecked Italian loafers. Burn the socks Tev wasn't using. Anything so Mal didn't have to come back here, to be devoured by a maw in the snow.

Just as he was thinking that, a crack sounded from overhead, and a limb came crashing down, almost on top of them. Tevyn was torn between dancing out of its way and seeing if Mal could get clear, when Mal gave a roar and launched himself on top of Tevyn, pushing him out of the way.

For a moment, Tevyn lay deep in the snow, breathless, Mallory on top of him, almost limp.

Tevyn shoved at his shoulder. "No sleeping yet!" he yelled. "C'mon, man, not this way!"

"Sorry," Mallory mumbled, struggling up. It took some doing, but finally they were upright, and Tevyn got a good look at the limb that had almost crushed them.

It was big, too big to break up with the bowie knife.

But if they fed it from under the fire blanket, through their fire pit, shoving more inside and peeling it as the other end burned down, it would last them at least two days.

"C'mon, Mal," Tevyn called, checking at the slack of rope they each had. "God, it can't be that far, I swear!"

Thirty feet, maybe. That's all it could have been. It felt like miles. Tevyn had come down mountain faces that hadn't been that long.

They pushed their find up against the rock face and slid down the rabbit hole back inside. The fire hadn't burned much more, but the snow was melted and boiling, and Tevyn could have cried. What had it been—ten minutes?

His entire life had passed before his eyes in ten goddamned minutes.

"Strip," he ordered Mallory sharply as he took off his parka and spread it back down on the mat of pine needles they'd slept on the night before. "Strip and sit down next to the fire. I've got a bottle of broth for you."

Mal grunted, and his suit jacket and pants hit the ground by the entrance. He bent over slowly to get them, but Tevyn beat him to it. "Just go sit down!" he cried, his voice wobbling. "Jesus, you scared the hell out of me. You were going to lie there and fall asleep, you bastard! Lie there and never get up!"

"I was too going to get up," Mal muttered, sounding drunk. "I was coming back to you. But I needed a nap first."

"What were you thinking, going out that last time! You were already tired. Mallory, you can't do that to me!"

"How's Damien?" Mal asked, surprisingly lucid.

Tevyn took a deep breath and tried to calm down. "His wound pussed—I think that's good. Means we're getting the infection out."

They both looked at Damie, sleeping now, breathing a little easier, the swelling in his leg having gone down even in the time they had been gone.

"It's less black," Mal said critically. "That's good. He's not as pale."

"Yeah. God. Stupid backwoods medicine. I had an ingrown toenail once, you know? Whole toe turned black with blood. Missy put my foot in a bucket of damned near boiling water. I screamed bloody murder, but…." He shrugged. His foot had been scalded and tender for the whole next day, but the infection had burst into the bucket.

"That's how you knew what to do," Mal said, admiration in his words. He shivered hard, and Tevyn grabbed the bottle of broth and came to sit down next to him.

"Here. I had mine. You missed lunch."

Mallory laughed weakly and drank. "Thanks," he said.

"Course."

"For saving my life out there."

"Purely selfish." Tevyn leaned his head against Mal's shoulder and swallowed against the aching in his throat. "Don't know your middle name yet. Would have driven me nuts."

Mal wrapped his arm around Tevyn's shoulders and turned, pulling Tevyn on top of him as he leaned backward against the branch behind them. "It's not Ambrose," he said as Tevyn shook against his chest. Part cold, part adrenaline—and part fear.

"Dammit," Tevyn mumbled, still shaking. "Arthur."

"Nope."

"Alexander."

"Nope."

Tevyn's brain stalled out. He was warm and alive, and Mal's chest was broad enough to rest on. "Don't let go for a few, okay?"

"I promise."

"I can't lose you."

"Yeah. I get that now."

"Good."

THERE was no more talk of going out after that. Mallory fell asleep, leaning back with Tevyn on his chest, and Tevyn squeezed his eyes shut and tried to find his center.

For the first time, he could see why Mallory and Damien had been against going out into the elements and trying to get down the mountain. Tevyn had grown up in the snow. He respected it, but he loved it a lot too, and it had loved him back for most of his life.

Mallory had grown up in the Bay Area—no snow there. Cold fog, yes, but wandering around the block in your bare feet wasn't often dangerous unless human predators were involved.

Damien was helpless. It looked like his fever had broken, and the infection had been pushed out, but he was exhausted, weak and shaky. Moving him like this would be a risk—but waiting for help to come before the infection set in again was a fool's gamble.

Nobody knew where they were.

*Nobody* knew where they were.

If they had gone hiking in the snow, they would have passed sign-in stations—small cabins or even wayposts, often fortified with supplies, with a ledger.

Those people Mallory had talked about, the ones who had burned everything and waited for rescue— they'd been hikers. They'd had a destination and let people know where they were going. They'd signed into wayposts on established paths.

Tevyn didn't doubt Damien had followed a flight plan, but he'd been in the process of deviating from it. A deviation like that, in the air, that was the difference between people knowing where you were and people finding your polished bones in a year.

In Tevyn's experience, nobody came back for you. Even if they were trying to, like Mal had been, the world opened up and swallowed you whole.

If you wanted to be found, you made yourself noticed—you flew down the hill faster, you did the best trick. You tied a rope to somebody and pulled yourself to them through the driving snow.

*I was coming back to you. But I needed a nap first.*

Tevyn's eyes burned behind his lids. Even covered in snow, a nap away from death, Mal had been thinking about him.

Intentions counted. So did degree of difficulty. Judges would give you better marks for trying a harder program and falling on your face than they would for trying a weak program any rookie could master.

Mal had been trying an advanced program in someone else's boots and in cashmere gloves, and he'd been doing it to save Damien's life.

Mallory had been planning to come back.

But Tevyn couldn't judge the rest of the world by the trust he put in Mallory Armstrong.

They were going to have to go find rescue themselves.


**MALLORY** slept that afternoon, and Tevyn tended to Damien some more. After a nap of his own, when the fire burned perilously low, he stoked the fire and went outside, making sure to tie their bedraggled T-shirt rope to the sapling—just in case.

All he was doing was dragging the limb around the shelter, to the other side where the fire sat, and digging a hole in the snow to feed the limb through. He'd gotten to the point where he'd lifted the fire blanket and shoved the cracked end of the wood through the hole left, when the wood suddenly took on a life of its own and jerked out of his hands.

"I've got it! Now get your ass in here and start stripping the bark!"

Tevyn almost jumped out of his skin. For some reason the blanket of snow, the fire blanket—it had all seemed so inviolate. It was hard to remember that their shelter consisted of a few layers of polymer and cold water.

"On my way!" he shouted back.

By the time he slid inside, he was shaking from exhaustion.

But Mal had started the water boiling again, and was stripping the old bandages from Damien's wound and putting a new set of hot ones on again. Damien was awake enough to bitch.

"Are you going to eat me when I'm done poaching? Just want a little warning."

"Are you kidding? We'd have to pound you and salt you and soak you in brine for you to be soft enough to eat. It's bad enough you look like you do, but you have to go for the washboard abs too? Bastard."

Damie's soft snort was reassuring. "You talk big, but I hit on you shamelessly, and you turned me down. Can't be that hot if you'd rather pine for Snow bunny here."

"He hit on you?" Tevyn asked, stripping off his parka. "Damien, you bastard. I *will* eat you!"

"Cool your jets," Damien breathed, apparently exhausted by simple conversation. "He's been in love with you since I've known him."

Mallory wrapped another hot bandage over the area, and Tevyn noted that it was looking very pink and decidedly scorched.

"We should let it breathe for a while and then pack it in ice again," Tevyn told him. He grimaced at Damien. "I'm guessing. You know that this whole thing is a guess on my part, about hot and cold and what it does to muscles and about trying to keep infection at bay."

"I'm breathing," Damien said, coughing softly. "I mean, that's gotta be worth something."

"Yeah, it means don't hit on Mal when we get back or I'll break your leg again."

Damien smiled, but he was apparently past talking. Mal was the one who broke the silence.

"He wasn't serious about it."

"Hitting on you?" Tevyn had thought that was all talk.

"He asked me out a couple of times."

"After Keith?"

"Yeah. I think I just looked sort of pathetic. Anyway"—Mallory patted Damien's arm—"his heart wasn't in it."

"And you were in love with me," Tevyn said. He met Mallory's eyes over the fire.

"And I was in love with you."

They stayed like that, eyes locked, until Damien cleared his throat. "Tevyn?" he said weakly.

"Yeah—you need that snowpack now?"

"No. I need you to listen to me really carefully."

"What?" Tevyn smiled at him, then was surprised when Damien didn't smile back.

"This guy here trying to poach me like an egg? He's a good guy. He gave my friend's business startup money when it was only a dream. He treats Preston like a real person, when most people sort of write him off because he barely speaks to humans. I will literally fly him to an island populated by naked cabana boys and leave him there until he's so sexed out he can't remember your name, if you break his heart. Do you understand me?"

"Damie, that's enough," Mal said quietly.

"No." Damien shook his head and touched Mallory's hand as he started to remove the bandages. "He needs to know. I wasn't half-hearted. I was serious. Your heart was already engaged. If he hurts you, I'm not the only one who'll line up to make it better." Damien sank back against his makeshift pillow. "I don't think I'll have to," he said. "But he needs to know."

"I know." Tevyn met Mallory's eyes and nodded so Mal would understand. "I know."

"Are we all uncomfortable now?" Mallory asked lightly. "Or should I give Damien a Vicodin so he's too stoned to have this conversation anymore?"

"I'll take the Vicodin," Damien said, sounding exhausted. "Just don't eat me."

"Not until we figure out Mallory's middle name," Tevyn told him. "Jory."

"Caspar," Damien countered.

"Samuel."

"Ezekiel."

"Are we doing biblical names?" Mallory asked. "Because I always wanted to be Nehemiah."

"Is it Nehemiah?" Tevyn asked sweetly.

"No."

"Then no. Abraham."

And so on.

By the time Mallory fell asleep, they'd packed Damien's leg with snow again and inflated the pressure bandage. Damien was stoned and asleep and exhausted— but his fever was down to unterrifying levels, and he was no longer sweaty and pale.

Tevyn had managed to pull the log through and skin at least half of it, and they'd started burning it as it sat in the fire. It was thick enough, and big enough, that their main worry was a spark flying up and catching in the low-hanging branches of the pine trees they were gathered under, but given the storm was still raging outside—and was still wet snow with big sleety flakes and not dry powder—that seemed unlikely.

Mallory had sat quietly during their guessing game and woven two more snowshoes, each one looking sturdier than the last. Tevyn had set them on the incoming log—close enough to the fire to cure, far enough away not to catch.

"I'll make some more tomorrow," he yawned, slouching down in his accustomed place now, next to Tevyn.

"Damien's not walking," Tevyn laughed.

"We need extra." Mallory regarded him soberly. "Unless we're really lucky, we're not going to find another shelter like this one. We need to have as much as we can carry to get us through."

Tevyn nodded. "If we get caught out around sunset, we can dig a hole in the snow. If we carry some fire starter and fuel with us, we can have a fire and keep melting ice for water."

So far they'd only used a few of the hand warmers when Mal had gone outside for firewood. Tevyn had plans for the rest.

"I'm thinking my trench coat for a travois," Mal murmured, surprising him. "We can do that quick sewing thing you did around some branches—it'll make it easier to haul Damien through the snow."

"Good idea." Tevyn's hands were full of sap from working on the log, but all of them were dirty and sweaty and covered in pitch. He stroked his fingers through Mallory's hair anyway because he needed to touch him and because it would comfort them both. "Let's talk about something else." The idea—*his* idea—of going out and finding rescue was terrifying to him right now. He'd won. Mallory had almost died today because he'd braved the elements, and he was still planning to do what Tevyn asked.

Tevyn needed a dream for when they survived, or he'd never get over the fear of leading them all to their deaths.

"What do you want to talk about?" Mal asked softly.

"I want a dog."

Mallory *hmm*ed. "Big? Small? Midsized?"

"Something that'll play in the snow. Something we can take to Missy's cabin in the summer."

"My mom's old dog was too small for that. Have you seen English Labradors? They're huge. Ginormous heads. Have that sort of patient, long-suffering look that makes you think they'll put up with your bullshit forever."

"Sounds perfect. He'd have to stay at your house. You'd have him when I traveled."

"But then I couldn't see you win." Mallory's voice took on a plaintive note, and Tevyn's hand stilled in his hair.

"Then you'd take him with you when you came to my events."

"He'd miss you when you went without us," Mal slurred. "But Charlie would dogsit. She misses dogs."

"And in the summers, you could work from the cabin," Tevyn told him, not caring if it was fair.

"I'll have better Wi-Fi cables installed this winter," Mal murmured. "Hire someone to fix it up."

He'd offered to do that before—and Tevyn had been all for it—but Missy had balked, not liking that someone she didn't know would be doing the work. But Missy wouldn't be there, and as much as Tevyn didn't like the idea of her being gone, maybe Mal thought this was a way to help him go on.

"They could replace the roof and the subflooring," Tevyn agreed. "Fix up the porch, fix the plumbing—"

"Seal the windows, update the electricity, add a big shower, a mudroom, some insulation in the roof and walls—"

Tevyn laughed. "You've got a whole list."

"I've wanted to fix that cabin since I first saw it," Mallory admitted. "I wanted it comfortable, for Missy. For you. My house used to be my mom's. I'd go home when she was alive, and she'd have a list of stuff for me to do. And I could do it because I had the weekend and a shitty love life. I couldn't do it for Missy. But I can do it for you."

"Your mom must have been so proud of you," Tevyn said, a lump in his throat. He thought of Mallory all alone, not much older than Tevyn was now. He'd survived. He'd been lonely but okay.

Tevyn would have Mallory in his life. He'd be okay. He had to remember that.

"Can I take you to the theater?" Mal asked, wandering from the topic. "We could dress up. You look good in a tux. Not all the time. Just once in a while. I could be a handsome prince, and you could be a handsome prince, and we could be Mr. and Mr. Handsome Prince before you go out to do battle on the slopes."

"I'd be proud to go to the theater with you," Tevyn whispered. "And we have to go dancing too. You're such a surprise as a dancer."

"Mm. Only with you."

Tevyn rubbed his back, between his shoulder blades. "Go to sleep, Mallory. Dream of dancing and theater—"

"And a little cabin in Colorado with new hardwood floors. And a giant dog who misses you."

"But loves you too."

"Okay. Are you sure he'll love me?"

Tevyn's heart hurt. "*I* do."

"Mm. Love you too. Night."

"Night."

He fell asleep, and Tevyn stayed still for quite a while, not even tempted to drop off with him.

Of course he loved Mallory Armstrong. There was no question.

God, they had to make it back home.

## *Daylight*

**TEVYN** woke him when the night seemed darkest, and Mallory took fire watch. He sang again, remembering as much as he could from his favorite shows, and sometime near dawn, after he'd just repositioned the big log and the shelter was lovely and comfortable, Tevyn spoke.

"You've got a real good voice, Mal. You need to sing in the shower or something when we get back."

Mal chuckled rustily, exhausted to his toes. "I'll try to remember. Note to self: Tevyn doesn't mind singing in the shower."

"I'm going to be listening," Tevyn promised. "Now lie down next to me and get some more sleep, okay?"

Such a gift. Mal had never realized how much of a gift giving sleep to someone who was exhausted could be.

He lay down in front of Tevyn again, and they both must have fallen asleep.

When Mal awakened, Damien was feeding another log into the fire to supplement the big one that had sunk to embers. The shelter was chilly in spite of the brightness of the sun glaring off the snow outside.

The brightness of the sun.

Mal sat up and began to help stoke the fire again, the better to consume the big log while they had it.

The fire stoked, he looked at Damien, who was pale but composed.

"How're you doing?"

"Better than yesterday," Damien admitted. They both looked toward the trench coat because it was the established door now, whether they liked it or not. "Not good enough to go out in the snow. Not today."

Mal nodded. "A day to rest," he said, his bones still weary from his near miss. God, he could remember thinking, *A nap. Just a nap.* It had sounded so reasonable in the middle of a blizzard.

"And then we can go out and freeze to death," Damien said grimly.

Mal shook his head. "Believe in him, Damie. I do. We're going to go find help. If nothing else, we can go find our cell phones, and help will find us."

Damien closed his eyes and nodded. "Get some more sleep, Mal. He's going to have all sorts of plans today."

Mallory turned his back toward the fire this time and pulled Tevyn against his chest.

*Believe in him.*

*Believe.*


**DAMIEN** was right about plans. They spent the day testing out the snowshoes and looking for branches big enough to work as a travois and small enough that they wouldn't kill Mal and Tevyn to pull behind them.

Two of the shoes fell apart completely before they were done with them, and one of them sustained minor damage. Mal figured he'd spend the evening rebinding them, but they had two complete pairs, sturdy and practical, that they used to go look for the travois branches—which they didn't find.

"This is ridiculous," Tevyn muttered, looking at the vast expanse of flat whiteness between the trees. "Yesterday we had half a tree *fall on our heads*, and now it's like, 'Wood? There's no wood here!'"

"We're in a forest, Tev," Mallory told him dryly, then held up his hands to Tevyn's glare. "Yes, you're right. I know what you mean."

"What're we going to do?" Tevyn asked seriously, and he did have a point. Damien's leg was still broken and he might be overcoming the infection, but walking was out of the question.

"Well, the fire blanket worked pretty well the first time," Mal pondered. "Let's use some of those T-shirt scraps to make handles with the ends, and maybe some of the rope to sew him into it."

"That's good," Tevyn said. "But what if it wears out. The thing with your coat is that it's sturdier."

"Well, maybe both? Sew him into the fire blanket, secure the fire blanket on top of the coat. Maybe turn the coat inside out so the satin's sliding on the snow and the wool's insulating him from it."

Tevyn nodded, and they stood for a moment in the sparkling white of the cold new day. "We should go look at the tree line," he said softly. "To get an idea."

Walking in snowshoes was harder than it seemed in the movies. Every step required coordinated muscle movement to lift the new attachment up and out of the snow and then to place it on top again. The snow sucked at the mesh, unwilling to give up this new object it could embrace, and although they'd secured the shoes with scraps of T-shirt at the toes, the better to shush-shush and slide forward, the temptation to lift the back too was almost overwhelming.

Mal was panting and sore by the time they reached the tree line and looked out over the edge of the world.

"I see nothing but canyon and other mountains," he said, swallowing hard.

"There has got to be something else out there," Tevyn muttered. "I mean, the railroad, Highway 80, Tahoe—we *know* they're around here somewhere!"

"Not from this vantage point." Mal took a deep breath and deliberately turned his body away from the great nothingness of wilderness that vaulted into space. "Okay, the one thing we can control. Downhill. We keep the edge of the mountain to our left—"

"East," Tevyn said. "That's northeast."

"So we're going southwest. Unless there's an airline, that's not what we're worried about now. We just keep going downhill and don't fall off the mountain. What's downhill?"

"The tree line keeps going," Tevyn mused. "That's good. We stick to the tree line so we can find shelter when we need to, but we stay on the edge so we're visible."

"We mark the trees as we go," Mal added. "Every hundred yards or so—scrap of cloth, carved initial, whatever—starting with this one here." He pointed to the last tree before the mountain flattened out to the cliff's edge. "Anyone searching for us can at least see we were there."

Tevyn nodded. "I…. God, I wish we had a tent."

"If we're wishing, wish for more food," Mal said, stomach growling. They had what? Two more days of broth and one more day of power bars. "I'd trade Damien in for a pastrami sandwich."

"You would not," Tevyn said, turning in toward the trees.

"I would too! Full-on sauerkraut and everything!"

"You'd eat chicken on whole wheat, no mayo, like you always do."

Mallory shook his head no. "Pastrami, on rye, special sauce and everything. This here would be a celebration sandwich."

"Well, if we're having celebration food, I want prime rib and lasagna."

Of course he would. "That's why I love you—you always think bigger."

Tevyn gave him an arch look. "Don't have to think. I *know* bigger."

Mal threw back his head and laughed, the sound bouncing off the snow and out into the canyon, and when he looked at Tevyn to make sure he was kidding and not being a douchebag, his laughter stilled.

Tevyn was biting his lip shyly, eyes crinkled, like a kid who'd done something wonderful but wasn't sure if the adults approved.

"What?"

"Your laugh. I… I don't know if I've ever heard you laugh like that. I made you do that."

Very carefully, Mallory shuffled the few steps between them, leaning over so they were close enough to touch. "You—in my entire life, nobody has ever made me feel like you do. I… I kept it inside. For a long time, I kept it inside. But what good will that do me today? What good will it be to keep it secret today when we're risking our lives tomorrow?"

Tevyn swallowed. "See? I should know that. I take risks every day. I should have known not to keep it inside. Why'd…. Why'd it take so long for this to happen between us, Mal? Why couldn't we have been doing this for the last five years?"

Mallory bit his lip. "Because you were young and flying down mountains, and I didn't want to steal that away."

Tevyn shook his head. "No. You're not taking a damned thing from me that I don't want to give you, twice over. It's because I was afraid. Five years, you stayed with me. I just needed to know you'd stay."

Mal kissed him, softly, barely keeping balance, and then pulled away. "If there's breath in my body, I'll stay."

Tevyn nodded. "If there's breath in my body, I'll always fly down the mountain to you."

The world hung breathless then, two tiny humans at the mercy of a lovely, merciless wilderness, small heartbeats on the crust of snow that threatened to swallow them into oblivion at any time.

But Mal could feel the warmth of Tevyn's breath, see flecks of green in his blue eyes, the impossible curve of his bottom lip as he bit down on it in shyness.

"Whether we make it down the mountain or not, Tev, we're gonna be forever."

Tevyn smiled then, all shyness banished. "I'm king of the goddamned hill, Mal. Don't worry about getting down the mountain. No one's ever offered me forever. I'm gonna grab it with both hands."

Bold words. And, like a blessing, they found a large downed limb with branch offshoots from it.

Wasn't big enough to use as a travois completely, but it *was* big enough to shove through the arms of Mal's coat to work as handles. The offshoots were good as walking sticks—which were actually needed to prod the snow in front of them, looking for holes like the ones Mal had fallen into.

"You know what the real irony of those holes is," Tevyn said in disgust.

"They're like premade snow caves, but because we fall into them they're going to kill us?"

"No! It's that they're usually caused by *branches* at the bottom, making the wind and the snow do weird things!"

Mallory chuckled. "So much irony in nature. I had no idea."

"Like the irony that now that we've finally stopped being stupid with each other, we're dirty, sweaty, and the closest we are to getting naked with each other is drawing each other's names in the snow when we pee?"

"Oh my God, you didn't!"

Now it was Tevyn's turn to chuckle. "I like how that horrifies you—like anybody but us would know!"

"*I'd* know!" Mallory told him, definitely horrified. "I mean, name in lights, yes! Name in *piss*, no!"

Tevyn gave a decidedly lascivious grin. "How about name in come? Because at this point, I could write you a love letter. How's that?"

The crudeness shocked him—but the thought of them, naked, raw, uninhibited, set him on fire. "Dammit!" he snapped because suddenly his whole body was tingling, not that Tevyn's suggestion was possible, but trying would be everything.

"Yeah?"

"Now we *really* have to get down this mountain!"

Tevyn was still laughing as they drew even with the shelter. "That's what I'm talking about! Incentive!"

They rested for the remainder of the day. Mallory spent part of his time fixing the ruined snowshoes—and reinforcing the ones that survived—and Tevyn used his knife and pieces of T-shirt to make handles for the travois.

"I figure I'll sew Damien onto the coat right before we take down the fire," Tevyn said thoughtfully. "We can leave about an hour after sunrise."

Damien nodded, still tired. "Since mostly what I'm gonna do is slide behind you, I really can't complain," he said.

"You need to tell us if you start getting feverish or nauseous," Mallory told him seriously. "If it starts hurting too much—whatever. We can't fix it if you just grin and bear it."

"Well, bitching is an unappreciated skill." Damien closed his eyes. "And seriously, how many more Vicodin do we have?"

"Enough to keep you stoned on an empty stomach for a good three days," Tevyn told him, and they all grimaced. "Lots of water, Damie. It's going to be back there with you. Let us know when it's time to add more snow."

Damien nodded. "I appreciate that you're trying to keep me alive and pain-free. If we can not be people-sicles by the end, I'm calling it a win."

It was a pact then, and to seal it, Mallory started singing "I'm a Nut," and they all joined in.

That night, after Damien had fallen asleep, Mallory leaned back against the bench and pulled Tevyn into his arms.

"Tell me more," Tevyn begged him.

"More what?"

"About you and me when we're down the mountain."

Mallory nuzzled his ear. He smelled like sweat—they both did—and while on a city street it would be unpleasant and rank, here, in this shelter, when they were safe and warm, it was simply an animal smell that was familiar to him now.

"You're going to qualify for the Olympics next year," Mallory said. "And depending on the rules, you can stay with me in the hotel. And at night, you can tell me how you're going to beat the next run, and you can play your music as loud as you need to, and you can use me any way you want if it's going to help you make the end of the run. And I'll be at the bottom waiting, and you'll hug Gretta and Harold and Sean—but you'll kiss me, and all the cameras will whirr, and we won't care."

Tevyn sighed and pushed back into his arms a little more.

"This is good," he said. "I'm going to have to teach you to snowboard, though."

Mallory snorted. "Good luck with that. Why?"

"So you can know how it feels. So you can go down the bunny hill and go 'booyah!' and when you see me do a trick, you'll know what that's like, even a little."

It was a good plan. Ambitious, but doable. "It needs to be a very small bunny hill," Mallory warned.

"Naw. The way you dance? You'll be a natural."

"Maybe take me sledding first." Mallory tightened his arms around Tevyn's waist.

"Like this," Tevyn said, leaning a little to the left. "And this." They leaned to the right. "And sit down hard and lean and it'll skid sideways and stop!" And they both did that on the hard dirt and needle floor of their temporary home.

"Ready for the bobsled event," Mallory laughed.

"Yup." Tevyn turned his head sideways, angling his body so he could rest his cheek against Mallory's chest. "Don't want to change you, Mal," he murmured. "Just want to take you with me."

"I'll go on whatever adventure I need to," Mallory told him. "However I get to stay." They were quiet, and Mallory suspected Tev was falling asleep.

"Sing to me. The one about hoping you get it."

So Mallory sang *A Chorus Line* until Tevyn was asleep, and took first watch. He woke Tev when he couldn't hold his eyes open, and they lay down together while Tev took second. He was fast asleep when Damien took the predawn shift, and when they woke up, the sun was shining into the shelter through the filtering branches of the trees.

It was time to go.


**IT** seemed like breakdown should have taken longer. Those flimsy blankets and Mal's trench coat had been their home for the last four days. But it took them maybe fifteen minutes to pack everything they had left—every scrap of fabric they'd cannibalized, every small element they hadn't burned. Tevyn kept the used-up hand warmers, putting some of them in their boots to keep their feet dry as they walked, and the others in with the cotton balls because the iron oxide could start a fire damned quick too.

He took one of the live ones and put it in the insulated first aid case with the two water bottles, both full of snow melted on their morning fire. "We have enough of these to keep us in water for the next three days, if we can melt our own at night," he told them. The battered tin box went in the go bag. Damien carried the water, and they draped the go bag over one of the handles of the travois. The fire blanket had threatened to tear when they'd tried to sew it to the trench coat, so they'd sacrificed one of the remaining T-shirts and two sets of briefs to lace Damien into the wool—using about half of their T-shirt rope to do it.

"I'm going to be peeing in that bottle until you cut me out of this thing," he'd muttered. It had let them make a double pad out of the fire blanket to wrap around his legs and gave him wool on his bottom, thighs, and back, with Mal's suit jacket jammed behind his shoulders to help support his head and neck.

He was as good as he was going to get, and the sun had risen enough to touch them in the depth of the tree line.

It was time to go.

Mallory took a good look behind him as they left their little cluster of trees and rock face. They'd dumped snow over their fire, and the remainder of the log appeared untouched as it arched out of the snow. They'd tucked all of the bark Tevyn had peeled into the go bag with their few remaining items, because it might smoke, but it could be used with the iron oxide to start an emergency fire.

Tev had taken a moment and carved their initials in the fallen tree they'd used as a bench on occasion, figuring it would hold their names until finding them no longer mattered.

They took off then, going as fast as the makeshift snowshoes would allow them, hauling Damien behind.

Within an hour, Mallory took off his sweatshirt and offered it to Damien, who was freezing without exertion to keep him warm. Tevyn's tight sweater was every bit as insulated as he said it was, and Tevyn slung his parka over the end of the travois as well. The work was hot and hard, and they stopped often to drink from the water bottles and replenish the snow to melt inside them. In the early afternoon, before the shadows grew long, Tevyn broke a protein bar into three pieces and made everybody eat. They were saving the last of their broth ration for that night.

The mountain itself seemed vast, as though their morning and noon trek had barely gotten them to the downward slope of it, and Tevyn tasked Damien with trying to figure out where they were.

"The wind was pretty sturdy at thirty knots when we took off," Damien said seriously over their lunch break. "But suddenly we hit that canyon, and the updraft kicked in around sixty. That's why I turned around. There's no beating that, not in a big tank of a commercial copter. I swear, those winds have gotten worse in the past few years."

Climate change—so terrifying on so many levels.

"So judging by the mountains around us...."

"About ten miles southeast of Donner Pass. There's probably a small town maybe five miles from the base of this hill, if we keep going south, and I think if we keep wandering east, we may—*may*—stumble across Highway 89, but no promises. Did I mention I was trying not to drop us out of the sky?"

Tevyn nodded grimly. "Understood. Bottom of the mountain, guys. There's just no way around it."

But the slope of the mountain seemed as likely to get them somewhere as the curve of the earth.

When the shadows started growing long, they went back into the slightly warmer area behind the tree line, searching for another friendly tree cluster for shelter—but no such luck. The temperature started dropping quickly as soon as the sun dipped behind the horizon, leaving Mal and Tevyn at the base of the biggest pine tree they could find, noting that the clearing of snow at its bole was about four feet lower than they were.

Mallory shivered and looked at Tevyn, who nodded soberly.

"Snow cave," he said. "You go down first and start digging. I'll get the metal box—you can use it to scoop out more room. We'll put one fire blanket underneath us, start the fire at the base of the tree so the smoke can escape, and use the other fire blanket to line the back of the cave. It's all we got. I'll fetch some firewood and start stomping down a slope on the other side so we can slide Damien down. Let's get to it."

Snapping the box in half felt like betraying a friend, but the metal definitely worked faster than Mallory's aching hands. While he worked, Tevyn stomped down a trail on the other side of the tree, dropping load after load of firewood that he stacked to Mal's left while Mal kept hollowing out more and more of the snowpack, leaving about a foot of it over their heads in a little arch and keeping the spot for the fire between the snow cave and the tree.

When it was big enough, after Mal had lined it with the blankets, Tevyn slid Damien down backward, and Mal caught him, hauled him back into the little cave, and started the fire as soon as he was situated.

The iron oxide helped, little sparkles emitting from the flames as they caught and burned the still-green bark. They set the rest of the packet aside—the storm had knocked a lot of branches down, but few of them had been dead before set upon by the wind.

Tevyn joined them after one last batch of firewood, and the three of them together huddled in the back of the cave, teeth chattering, waiting for the warmth to kick in.

When they were warm enough to remember it, Damien reached into the insulated bag and pulled out one of the thermoses of melted water. Tevyn added their second-to-last packets of broth mix to it, and they shared it like a flask.

Damien took a sip and muttered, "This just reminds me that I haven't had enough really good scotch in my life."

Tevyn took it from him. "Beer. IPAs—the good ones. When the company is big enough to know what they're doing, not big enough to be bought out by a bigger company."

Mallory took his drink and played the game. "Crisp white wine," he said. "A little fruity, but not too much. With a plate of chicken carbonara."

"Talisker," Damien said on a sigh. "After lobster for dinner."

"Fat Tire," Tevyn finished. "Thirty-two-ounce porterhouse, medium rare, mushrooms, and a loaded baked potato."

For a moment they enjoyed the warmth of the liquid—and of the fantasy. Mallory knew that fantasy by now, knew how important it was to give their minds something to do besides dwell on the warmth and the food and the safety they didn't have.

"There is this dance club in the Haight," he said, and Damien chortled.

"*You*, go dancing in the *Haight*?"

"Once or twice," Mallory said with dignity. "After a bad breakup. When my self-esteem was really low and I thought, 'Hey, maybe someone will appreciate a man in a three-piece suit.'"

"Wait a minute." Tevyn regarded him suspiciously. "Was this where you picked up that porn model? The one who said you hit high C?"

Mallory laughed. "Same place—probably same night. The thing is, dance clubs aren't supposed to serve food. And if they do, it's supposed to be, like, pizza bites from a tiny toaster oven powered by hamsters in the back, right?"

Damie and Tevyn looked at each other and nodded, as though they agreed that yes, this was dance club cuisine.

"Well, this place—it was an old rave warehouse, and I don't even know if it's still there, but nobody had told them their food was supposed to be shitty. They made these hamburgers that were *amazing*. I mean, for all I know they laced them with Viagra, which could explain the whole Skylar episode, but all I remember was that I was drinking cheap vodka and I asked for a burger, and what showed up on my plate was haute cuisine, with some of the best kettle-cooked chips I have ever tasted. If this was a hamster-powered toaster oven, it was *magic*."

"So you're saying you should give up because you'll never have that burger again?" Tevyn asked, sounding appalled.

"No! I'm saying that some of the most magical things happen when you're someplace you never expected to be, with people you didn't expect to spend time with." He caught Tevyn's eyes across Damien and winked.

"Like me," Tevyn said, getting it.

"Like us."

"Are you trying to make me puke?" Damien asked. "Because it's terribly unfair to have this conversation when I'm *sewn into my bed*."

"Yeah, Damie," Tevyn muttered. "That's why we hauled you across the damned mountain. So you could throw up on us when we can't even run away."

"*Half* the damned mountain," Damien muttered. "Which is the only reason I'm saving you from the finale of the show."

His voice sank on a note of misery, and Tevyn and Mal moved in a little closer to him, huddling under Tevyn's parka.

"You two sleep first," Mallory said softly. "I'll mind the fire."

"I can't even help with that here," Damien said. "And I shouldn't be this tired. All I did was get my ass dragged across the snow!"

"Damien, you're sick," Mallory said brutally. "Get some sleep. When it's your turn, you can wake one of us when the fire's low. C'mon, man. Keep thinking about scotch and steak. We'll get there."

"Yeah." Damien yawned. "Yeah." He fell asleep soon after, and Tevyn reached across him to grab Mal's hand.

"It was a rough day," he said, sounding dispirited.

Mallory squeezed his hand. "And yet we're still alive."

Tevyn smiled slowly. "You're handy to have around, Mallory Fitchner Armstrong."

"Yes, I am, and no, that's not it."

"Crispin."

"No."

"Ian."

"No."

"Joel, Joey, Joseph, Joe?" he tried.

"Noel, Noey, Noseph, and No!" Mal fired back, overjoyed when he laughed.

"Gabriel," Tevyn suggested, eyes bright as they regarded each other in the confines of the cave, the fire their only salvation. "Like an angel."

"Nope. Just Mallory. Like a man."

"*My* man."

"If you'll have me."

Tevyn nodded and then leaned his head against Damien's chest, because there was no more room anywhere else. "I will."

Mal fed some more green branches into the fire, grateful for a wind that pulled the smoke away from them—and that they couldn't feel in their snug little cave. When the fire was satisfactory, he set up the two halves of the metal box with snow to melt, because their water bottles needed to be replenished.

They'd been gone for five days. They'd *survived* for five days. One way or another, this thing was drawing to a close.

# *Finding Wings*

**THE** next day dawned overcast—not threatening snow, but no sun to warm them as they trudged through it either. Mal worked hard to keep their spirits up, but Damien spent a lot of time huddled in misery, helpless, and, in spite of their best efforts at medication, in pain.

Tevyn was feeling the effects of hunger. Without exertion, if they were someplace warm, they could survive for another five days on water alone. But he and Mal were working their asses off, stomachs grumbling, their rationed half a power bar and broth just enough to put one foot in front of the other.

And even that was running out tonight.

The fuzzy gray disc of the sun dipped toward the horizon, and the temperature dropped. Tevyn glanced at Mallory, who had the same look he'd worn since the helicopter had gone down. The one that said he'd do anything necessary to be there for Tevyn, anything Tevyn would ask.

Tevyn couldn't ask any more of him. Not today. "We need to find shelter!" he called, hoping for more than a hole in the snow tonight. "Maybe with some more time we can find something better!"

Mallory nodded, and together they turned and trudged back to the tree line, Tevyn stopping to mark trees every so often as they went.

He'd been doing that on the way down—every two hundred yards or so, he'd leave a scrap of used bandage on an overhanging tree limb, or scratch an arrow pointing the direction they were heading in on a tree trunk, if one was close enough.

Anything to mark that they'd been there, in case he was making the wrong goddamned call.

Which was exactly what it felt like as they stumbled through the forest, heading toward the center of the mountain. Tevyn hoped the extra time would buy them a chance to get near the rocky outcropping that had served as a wall originally, helping to shelter them all from the wind, but the drop in temperature made him start eyeing tree trunks again, wondering which one would help them make another snow cave like the night before.

"Hang on," Mallory said. Making sure Tevyn saw what he was doing, he set his end of the travois down, and Tevyn joined suit. Their backs and arms were exhausted and trembling—Tevyn knew if his were, Mallory's had to be too.

"Where you going?"

Mal was heading for a mound in the snow, next to what looked like a fallen tree, leaning on its fellows.

"That looks wrong," Mallory said, nearing the mound suspiciously. He was about five feet away from it when he dropped completely out of sight.

"*Shit*!" Tevyn ran toward the mound but stopped short of where Mal dropped out of view, and heard a knocking sound.

A hollow, metallic knocking.

And Mallory swore, long and creatively, using the synonym for fornication in amazing and creative ways.

"Mallory? Holy shitballs, man—what's got you so riled!"

"Tev, it's a *plane*! An old one! Under the snow!"

Tevyn lay down on his stomach and crept forward to peer over the lip of the hole Mallory had fallen down.

And gasped.

"Oh wow. What is that? Four passengers maybe?"

"Mm…." Mallory was peering in through a window. "Yeah. I'm thinking a Cessna 182. There's no wing…." He squinted above them at what Tevyn had first thought was a tree. "Or, well, it's not attached to the plane anymore."

Tevyn stared at it and then back to Mallory in the hole in the snow. "Is the, uhm…." *Oh, how grisly.* "Is the pilot still there?"

Mallory peered inside again and shook his head. "No. In fact, the cockpit door is frozen open—see?"

Tevyn had to squint against the encroaching darkness. "So, think we can get Damien down there?"

Mallory nodded. "Go get him. I'll try to make a ramp. But first… hey. I've got an idea. Give me one of the used-up hand warmers and the flint striker. I want to make sure nothing else has decided to use this as a home!"

Tevyn had both items in his pocket, so he handed them over. Then he ran back to the travois for more iron oxide packets and found Damien tiredly kvetching about having the world's shittiest view.

"What in the hell—"

"Look, we might actually have shelter tonight. And some more resources. So give me the first aid kit and hang tight!"

"C'mon, Tevyn, could you at least drag me a little closer so I can hear you talk?"

Tevyn took a deep breath and remembered that while he and Mallory got to exchange looks as they dragged the travois behind them, all Damien had was a stunning view of the sky, with his own snail trail in the snow for variety.

"Yeah, sure. But not too close. Don't want you to go sliding down into that hole without help."

"Understood."

It was a good thing the bottom of that coat was slicker than K-Y on a stainless steel rod—it was difficult to haul by himself but not impossible.

When he got back, Mallory had already started a fire inside the airplane, back in the cargo area near the tail.

It was burning merrily, consuming what looked like a pile of debris that was inside the plane, and Mallory was near the tail end—part of which had broken off— scraping down snow to give Damien a ramp.

"If we pull the handle out of the travois, we can slide him down in here and let him get warm while we go get wood for the fire," Mal said excitedly. "There were old bird's nests and branches in there. The windows on the other side are broken, and the whole thing is tilted so they're near the ground. But I didn't see any snakes or raccoons or anything, and I don't smell cat piss, so I don't think there's a mountain lion here."

They'd seen one that day, around noon, walking on the fringes of the tree line, eyeballing them with prejudice—but not attacking.

A few moments later, they'd heard a tussle back among the trees and a high-pitched squeak. Tevyn had pitied the poor bunny, but figured better Mr. Cottontail than the three humans who didn't have a whole lot of fight left in them.

"Awesome. I'll lower him down backward. You drag him in. Ready to get out of the cold for a bit, Damie?"

"God, yes," Damien muttered. "Don't suppose there's anything soft there for my back?"

"We got ourselves a jump seat!" Mal said, pointing to it with a little bit of glee. "Are we ready?"

They made it sound cheerful, and in a way it was. Warmth. Actual seats. A true shelter from the wind.

But Tevyn's limbs were aching with exhaustion, and he knew Mallory must be about done. Damien had been a trouper, but the lines of pain were etched so tightly around his forehead, eyes, and jaw, Tevyn was surprised he hadn't cracked a tooth, trying not to cry out every time they went over a bump. And while they were getting closer to the bottom of the mountain, they weren't getting there fast enough. Tevyn estimated they had two more days of hiking just to get down there, and they'd eaten the last of their food that morning.

And the hand warmers were almost all gone, so they'd be hoping Damien's body heat would keep the water melted for the next couple days too.

So Tevyn lowered Damien into the defunct airplane, knowing very well it might be their final resting place—in the darkest sense of the word.

Shortly thereafter he was giving Mallory a hand up the ramp, and they were slogging through the snow again, looking for wood.

Out of curiosity, Tevyn led them toward the wing, propped up against the nearby tree. Or, well, half a wing.

"I wonder where the other half is," he said, pushing at the fifteen feet of aluminum alloy to see how strongly lodged it was. There were two half-corroded struts on the bottom, but he figured they could break that thing off and….

*And what?*

"Back in the forest somewhere." Mal got on Tevyn's side of the thing and pushed at it, hard. Together they managed to dislodge the broken half from the snow, and it fell with a soft whump.

And skidded, belly first, only catching on the strut.

Tevyn caught his breath, the thought inevitable, and then he and Mallory locked gazes.

"Tell me I'm crazy," Tevyn said bluntly.

"I'm not sure we can make it two more days," Mallory replied, just as bluntly.

"This—this idea—this is dumb. Like… like insanely dumb. Like stupid TV people yelling at the screen saying, 'Don't do that, asshole! It's really frickin' dumb!'"

Mallory swallowed and moved toward the wing, then pulled hard until it was convex side down. The rounded side actually slid better, and he used the strut to push it along the icy crust of snow for a few feet and then let go.

And it kept going.

He turned to Tevyn, face tense. "Tev, we've got three choices. You know that, right?"

"You're the guy who does risk assessment for a living, money man—lay it out for me."

"The first is, we get up tomorrow and we keep hauling Damien down that hill."

They both shuddered. Damien's bid to be near their voices was about the only thing he'd asked for all day.

"We haven't changed the bandage in two days," Tevyn said, voice shaking. "I don't know how much longer he can make it."

"I don't think it's two or three days," Mallory told him, not backing down from the hard thing.

"What's the other choice?" He knew. It didn't even have to be a question.

"We go inside that plane, and we hunker down and mark trees and burn everything and live on snow and the peanuts I found when I was looking for paper to burn."

"There's peanuts?" Tevyn said hopefully.

"Well, yeah. They were going to be a surprise."

"We'd die there," Tevyn told him, all of the play gone from his voice.

"I know it. One night we'd let the fire go out and we wouldn't wake up." It had been in the tens or twenties every night since the helicopter crash. They had maybe three more weeks until the spring weather picked up.

"Now tell me the third option." Tevyn took a shaky breath. "I need to hear you say it."

Mal's lips curved up, just a little. "Well, Tevyn Moore, snowboarding superstar, we could strap ourselves to that big frickin' snowboard and let you fly us down this mountain."

Tevyn bit his lip, but he couldn't control the smile that wanted to escape.

"Wouldn't be dying slow," he said.

"Would be a helluva ride."

They both nodded, and without another word, turned toward a pile of fallen branches beyond the airplane wing. Their snowshoes were about disintegrated, only the most basic framework of branches remaining to keep them from sinking to their asses in snow.

"We have to ask Damien first," Tevyn warned.

"Please. He'll be pissed he didn't think of it."

And he was.

He was also, it turned out, really very excited about the little foil-wrapped packages of peanuts that Mal produced from a compartment in the cockpit. And even more excited about the pretzels behind them.

**THAT** night as Damien slept, Tevyn curled up in front of Mallory on the floor of the cargo area. The fire danced on the floor near the broken section of tail. The door was frozen open, but their tattered fire blanket made a decent wall for what they hoped was the final time.

For a moment, they were quiet, the conversation exhausted out of them, and then Tevyn rolled in Mallory's arms, coming face-to-face with him.

"What?" Mallory asked, voice so low Damien probably couldn't have heard him if he was awake.

"I just… just wanted to say something," Tevyn whispered. "Important. Because you and me, we've been dancing around each other for five years. And now, when we might not have any time at all, we've stopped dancing *around* each other and started dancing *with* each other. And I want you to know, if this was what it took for us to find this thing we've got?" He put his hand on Mallory's heart. "It was worth it. My whole life I might not have known this was real. And even if my life's cut short, knowing it was real? That's what makes it worth living."

Mallory made a suspicious noise, and the light from the fire was enough to reveal the silver tracks down the side of his nose.

"What?" he asked, worried.

"I was just going to say I love you."

Tevyn laughed. "That's plenty." And then he kissed him, hard enough to make Mallory open his mouth and groan, and Tevyn kept kissing until they were both liquid and aching and needy.

"Why?" Mallory muttered, burying his face against Tevyn's neck and arching his hips. "Why would you do that here?"

"'Cause that was a really fancy speech I gave," Tevyn told him, making sure his lips brushed Mallory's ear. "But I want to live. I want to live so we can do that clean and naked until we literally can't move anymore." He thrust his hand between them and squeezed Mallory through his sweats and his suit pants and briefs, and Mallory groaned.

"You suck."

"Oh yeah. I really do. I'm *great* at it. And we're gonna live to find out."

Mallory's tortured laughter was music to his ears.

**THEY** took shifts and let Damien sleep. When Tevyn awakened from his own slumber, he found that Mallory had taken his bowie knife and liberated all of the seat belts from the passenger compartment, including the ones from the child's jump seats on the side. As Tevyn woke up—part of an operations manual burning with the branches they'd found, the better to make the flames bright—the first thing he saw was Mallory, working hard with the bowie knife and some of the T-shirt rope, stitching the ends together tightly.

"Good idea," Tevyn mumbled, not quite ready to wake up.

"Go back to sleep," Mallory told him gently. "I'm not ready to let go of this project yet."

Tevyn did just that. Mallory woke him maybe an hour before dawn, the fire freshly stoked and burning warmly.

"Sun'll be up in a few," he mumbled, sliding under Tevyn's parka, which they'd been using as a blanket.

"Sleep in," Tevyn told him. "We leave after breakfast."

"Peanuts and pretzels—hooray!"

Tevyn kissed his forehead and took his position in front of the fire.

And prayed.

## *Flying*

**MALLORY** woke up with a start in the full light. "Oh my God. The fire—"

"Is fine," Damien said, feeding it another crumpled page from another useless manual. "Tevyn was out at first light, and he asked me to let you sleep."

"How are you?" Mallory asked, grateful Tev wasn't there because Damien tended to be honest when he wasn't trying to impress Tevyn.

"My leg's starting to hurt like a motherfucker," Damien said. "And I'm getting feverish again."

"We've got one more Vicodin," Mal said, just as honest. "And we used the last of the ibuprofen yesterday."

Damien nodded. "Let's save the pain pill until we strap me to the airplane wing. Any idea how we want to do that?"

Mal shook his head. "Prone?"

Damien winced. "I'll be helpless!"

"Yeah, but Tev and I will be riding it like a sled. You can't do that, not with your leg like it is. Keeping it immobile might be the only thing that's kept you alive!"

Damien grunted. "You know, six years in the Navy, I didn't get shot down once, didn't get wounded, didn't even get shot at. Here I am, on the biggest actual adventure of my life, and I'm strapped to the back of an airplane wing and hoping I don't get my skull crushed?"

Mallory sighed and looked around the plane again, noting the foam rubber padding coming loose from the seats.

"Actually," he said, "I've got an idea."

By the time Tevyn came back in, exultant and happy, a very unhappy Damien was sporting some very awkward headgear.

"Seriously?" he snapped. "It smells like pee! And you anchored it to my head using the waistband of Tevyn's jock!"

"And it's *brilliant*!" Tevyn crowed, excited. "Do I get one?"

"We all do."

Helmets. Not pretty—and yeah, the smell was something extra special—but Mallory's big fear about being strapped to the back of an airplane wing and flying down the hill was head injury.

This wasn't perfect, but it just might do.

"All right, guys," Tevyn said as he put his helmet on and ripped the last of the elastic from the jock to anchor it the same way Mallory had for Damien. "Let's go set the hill on fire."


**DAMIEN** was strapped to the back of the wing, feet first, head pillowed not only on the helmet, but on Mal's suit jacket as well. The seat belts had done the trick, but they'd used up a lot of rope making sure his head and neck were stabilized, and then they'd wrapped the bedraggled trench coat over him to keep him warm.

Mallory sat in front of him, legs spread to accommodate Tevyn. Tevyn belted them both together to the wing. He held a piece of wing strut in each hand, and Mal held the broken halves of the handle they'd used in the trench coat as the travois, so they could steer.

They'd set up near the airplane so they could practice shoving the thing through the snow like a gondola, and Mallory had to admit, even going sideways, it was a little easier than hauling a travois. But it wasn't until they cleared the tree line and turned the thing downhill that Mallory really appreciated the speed.

"One! Two! Three!" With a heave they started the thing downhill, and for a moment, Mallory held his handles aloft, waiting to see if he'd need to stop or push some more.

And then gravity took over.

*Whoosh!*

Just like a sled, they started speeding down the hill—but not straight. "*Lean right*!" Tevyn shouted as they made up for the unbalanced bottom of the wing.

Mal did, engaging his core and his obliques to compensate for the angle of the slide, and they continued to rocket down the hill. The wind whistled outside their makeshift helmets, and Tevyn yelled, "Put the sticks in your lap, Mal, and hang on!"

Mal did what he said, wrapping his arms around Tevyn and listening to his body. They saw a rock coming up, jutting out of the snow like a quick approaching nightmare, so Tevyn screamed, "Right!"

They leaned farther to the right, and their sled swerved, and Tevyn screamed, "Up!" and now they were going straight down again.

Left! Right! Straight! Down, down, down, so damned fast. Mallory's heart pounded in his throat and his blood thundered in his ears. He held tight to Tevyn Moore, who was the one thing in his life worth holding, and together they hurtled down the mountain, shouting in exhilaration.

"Oh shit!" Tevyn yelled. "Shit! We can't stop in time!"

Ahead of them was a great gap of maybe thirty feet, a divot in the mountain, and Mallory's heart froze.

"Head down!" Tevyn yelled. "We're going over!"

Mallory closed his eyes, the world dropping out from under them as they sailed through the air. He opened them when he felt the jarring of impact.

"Damien!" he hollered.

"Still here!"

And the sled hurtled on.

The terrain leveled out, still snowy but flat, and right when Mallory thought, *Hey, did we really get to the end of the mountain?* he saw the muddy service road, and he and Tevyn leaned hard to their right.

Their sled skidded to a halt, the bottom grinding on gravel as the snow disappeared, and they tumbled into the slush by the side of the road just as a Forest Service truck passed in front of them.

A Forest Service truck?

"Oh my God!" Tevyn laughed. "Oh my God! Damien! Damien, you okay?"

"Ouch," Damien mumbled. "Ouch. Shit. Crap. My head. My neck. My leg. That was awesome. I'm dead."

Mallory and Tevyn scrambled off the wing to help Damien out of the snow, only vaguely aware of the knot of people approaching.

And the dogs.

One of them, a giant pit bull crossed with something else, gave a distinctive bay. "Preacher?" Damien mumbled, and the dog broke loose from his handler and came to get in everybody's way and make sure Damien was okay. "Preacher?" he said again. "Where's Preston, buddy? Where'd he go—"

"Damien?"

Mallory and Tevyn looked up to see a gorgeous, blond, turquoise-eyed Adonis barreling through the rescue workers and drawing near. "Damien?" he asked, voice rusty, and Mallory managed to take the makeshift helmet off Damien's head before Preston got there.

"Thanks," Damien whispered.

"Got your back," Mallory whispered in return. "Preston!" he called. "Preston, he's fine!"

And then the rescue workers converged on them, shocked and excited that the missing passengers and pilot they'd been searching for had just blundered into their midst.

Mallory tore off his own helmet, and Tevyn his, and they had to be separated before the search and rescue people could take their vitals and hear their story and feed them hot soup and vitamin water.

They didn't let go of each other's hands unless they absolutely needed to.

Nobody even bothered to try to make them.


**IN** a remarkably brief time, they were seated in a passenger helicopter, wrapped in wool blankets, and nursing—oh God—more hot protein broth while Preston and a pretty blonde EMT named Jeri tended to Damien. Preston and Jeri spoke in brief, clipped medical shorthand, and every so often, Preston Echo would send Mallory and Tevyn covert glances with big turquoise eyes.

Preston's brother, Glen Echo, was piloting the copter and grilling Mal and Tevyn over the headsets.

"Bet you're glad you sprang for the luxury emergency suite, right?" Glen asked, and Mallory grinned tiredly. It was, in fact, a repurposed and refurbished Army surplus Black Hawk passenger transport. Glen had painted the entire thing eggshell white and put a very spiffy turquoise-and-red logo on the side of the tail—*Gecko Emergency Services*—and yes, the inside was comfortable, leather upholstered, and genuinely welcoming.

"Money well invested," he said. "Where are we going?"

"UC Davis Medical Center," Glen told him. "I know there are hospitals between here and there, but Jeri says the break is pretty bad and he's going to need surgery and super-strength antibiotics ASAP. He's stable enough to get him to a specialist, so that's what we're gonna do."

Mallory knew Glen and Damien had served together, and he heard the stout defense of a brother in Glen's voice.

"He was so strong," Mallory said, making sure Preston could hear him. "We dragged Damie all over the damned mountain, and he didn't so much as whimper about the pain."

"That there's a lie," Glen said dryly. "He's a snarky bastard, and I'm sure he let you have it."

"Well, yeah—but self-pity is not on his plate."

"No, it is not," Glen agreed. "And thank you. More specifically, thank you for dragging his sorry ass down the hill. Why did you do that, by the way?"

"You don't leave a friend behind!" Mallory protested indignantly.

Glen's voice softened. "I know you wouldn't, Mal. And now I know that about Tevyn. I meant why did you decide to come down the hill? Common wisdom says stay put."

"Our phones went over with the helicopter," Mallory responded. "Nobody knew where we were. We found shelter, waited out the storm, and started down. But we weren't going fast enough, and…." He couldn't say it. Not now, when Damien was warm and being tended to and answering the two EMTs with snark and succinct suggestions.

"He wasn't going to make it," Glen deduced. "You got on the back of that airplane wing because Damien couldn't wait."

"Well," Mallory said, catching Tevyn's eye. "In fairness, neither could Tev. You guys know me. I'm the king of hanging out and waiting for my chance. But Tevyn was going to gnaw his own leg off if we tried to keep him still."

Tevyn raised a shoulder and then leaned his head against Mal. He was on coms too—but much like after he'd run a competition, he needed an hour or two to decompress.

"Either way, I appreciate it. You brought our friend down the mountain—that's huge. And the fact is, even if we'd known you were up there, we couldn't have gone to get you."

"I'm sorry?"

"You guys were probably too close to see, but the entire top of that mountain is an avalanche waiting to happen after that last storm. Me and Preston had to throw a full-sized tantrum to get the local agencies to even spend time in that area. But we saw the empty copter and knew you three must have walked away somehow. It makes a lot more sense that Damien landed on that mountaintop and the copter slid off." He shuddered. "What was left when it hit bottom wasn't pretty."

"We're so glad you were there," Mallory said numbly. Lucky. They were so lucky. His arm tightened around Tevyn's shoulders. You couldn't rely on luck to have people you loved in your lives. From here on out, he and Tevyn were going to have to make their own luck.

"So I let Damien's parents know he's been found and is on the way to surgery. Is there anybody you want to call? Jeri's got a cell phone for you, if you know the number."

Jeri grimaced on hearing that and rather than taking off her sterile gloves, where she was doing important work, presented her backside instead, where her phone showed in a clear outline.

"Thanks," Mallory said. "That's, uh, kind." He laughed, but he took the phone and called Charlie, knowing the number by heart.

"Please tell me this strange number is Mallory. Mallory? That better be frickin' you."

"It's like you're psychic," he said weakly. "Did our company go under without me?"

"No, but you got a stunning number of people saying, 'Charlie, we trust you with our money, but how is our financial officer?' It's *scary*. You got *cards*, Mallory. Cards!"

Mal chuckled. "Maybe don't read them. Some of them probably say 'We needed you to sell stock when you were gone, damn you, and now it's dropped!'"

"No." Her voice grew thick. "Just no. I had to call
Glen to even talk to the sheriff's department. I've been
worried sick—don't *do* that to me, dammit! Without
you, Mal, I have no excuse to avoid my mother twice
a month. You're the only person on the planet keeping
me from jumping out a window!"

Her mother was very nice but *very* overbearing.
Mallory got it. "Love you lots too," he said fondly. "It's
good to know I'd be missed."

"God, you had to go and make it real. I love you
too. Now what can I do for you? There's got to be
something I can do."

Tevyn was so relaxed against him. "They're going
to want to check us out at the hospital, maybe keep us
overnight and give us fluids." He would almost rather
an IV than any more protein broth. "After that, we're
going to need a hotel near the hospital for at least one
night—"

"Why for?"

He could picture her, boy-cut short dark hair
tucked behind her ears, big gray eyes shrewd, full lips
pursed. She liked to wear slim-skirted power suits in
outrageous colors with black or white shells as a foil
underneath. She was stunning—not being able to make
it work with her had pretty much cemented Mallory's
gayness as incontrovertible fact.

"So we can see how Damien is."

"He's not okay?" Her voice squeaked. Everybody
loved Damien.

"He was hurt in the initial crash. He's going to
need surgery and antibiotics and probably more of the
above. But Tev and I are going to want to see how
he's doing, and then we're going to need to fly to
Colorado."

"So three hotel rooms," she mumbled.

"Three?"

"I'm coming!" she snapped. "At least until you go see how his grandma is." He'd told her why he'd gone up to Donner Pass in the first place—it was hard to remember. "What are you going to wear, Mal, scrubs? I'll go to your apartment and get you some jeans or something—"

"Buy some clothes for Tevyn—men's medium, twenty-eight-inch waist—"

"Twenty-six," Tevyn said softly, winking, letting him know he was still listening.

"Enough for a couple of days. Grab my suitcase from the closet. And we only need two hotel rooms. And one by the hospital in Colorado."

"One room," she said carefully, "for the two of you."

"Yes, Charlene, one room. For two consenting adults."

He heard a suspicious noise in his other ear and realized he hadn't turned off his com while he had this conversation. *Well, hell.*

"Three rooms in Sacramento," she said, voice flinty. "Two in Colorado."

"And you can eat the deposit," he snapped.

"You will thank me later!" she shrilled back.

"Charlie, don't be silly. You've seen this coming for five years!"

"But I hoped it wouldn't!" He heard her deep breath. "C'mon, Mallory. You almost died—"

"And now I know why I'm alive," he said, wheedling. "C'mon, Charlie. I'm grown. Have some faith. I bet Timmy is crazy about this idea."

She grunted. "Timmy knows I'm the brains of our outfit. Two rooms. I'll get two queens. For the two queens that'll be sleeping there. That's you and me, in case you didn't know what I was talking about."

"People on the street watching you have this conversation know what you were talking about, sweetheart. Thanks for doing this. Call this number when you get back into town—oh! And get me a cell phone and put it on the company account!"

She snorted. "Anything else?"

"Call Missy's hospital—"

All of her animation faded. "I've been calling every day since the helicopter went down. She's fading fast, Mal. I'll have your tickets out of Sac for the day after tomorrow."

"Thanks, honey."

"God, Mal, if you lost your heart to that kid in the frozen freaking wasteland, I'm cutting him off our Christmas card list."

"My heart's in good hands, Charlie. Trust me."

"You? With my life. A snow bunny with a case of hero worship? Hardly."

"I'm no hero—it must be the real thing."

She snorted. "I'll believe it when I see it. I'll buy his clothes, but I'm not buying his line. Don't argue with me—just go get checked out and okayed and make sure Damien lives to snark again. Now why couldn't you have come back in love with him? Don't answer that. It'll only depress me. I'm glad you're back, Mal. Don't piss me off."

She hung up, and Mal fought against a yawn before looking up the number of the hospital in Colorado.

"She didn't sound happy," Tevyn said softly.

Mallory shrugged. "She's protective. We went to school together. My mom died, and we started a new business. For a while it was us sharing an apartment

above our dinky little office building. Nobody's good
enough, you know?"

"And you were lovers," Tevyn reminded him.

Mal let out a little laugh. "Believe me, that's not
what's at work here. She's got a very hot, very attentive
piece of beefcake of her own."

"Then why—"

Mallory put his finger over Tevyn's lips. "I told
you—she's protective. She liked Keith, and we broke
up because I was in love with you. Because she watched
me for five years, comparing every guy I met to you.
She liked Damie, and I told him no."

"Because of me."

"Because of how I felt about you. You haven't
ruined my life, Tevyn." He pulled out a smile—one
that felt like it might even warm the permafrost in his
feet. "In fact, I think you saved it. Like, demonstrably.
Earlier this morning, remember?"

"Speeding down a hill?" Tevyn arched his
eyebrows. "I think I was there."

"Yeah. Give her time."

"As long as she gives us the hotel room," he said
darkly.

Mallory nodded. "Now I've got one more call to
make. Give me a minute."

It took ten. Mallory had to shake Tevyn awake to
connect him with his grandmother.

"Grandma? Yeah. It's me. How you doing?" Tevyn
grimaced. "Honey, they said you broke your hip. No,
they're not lying. Honey, they're—" His eyes got big,
and he covered the mouthpiece and whispered, "She
would have slapped me for those words!" Then, back
into the phone, "I'm coming, Missy. No, not today. I
have a flight out of Sacramento in two days. I'll come

then." The voice on the other end got sad and quavery, and Mallory tightened his hold on Tevyn's shoulders. "I know you're confused, honey. I'll be there as soon as I can be. Yeah, Missy. I raced real good. I raced so good, I put Mallory on the back of my board and he came down the hill with me."

Whatever Missy said next, it made Tevyn sit up straight and catch his breath.

"Yeah, Missy. He *is* a good man. You're right. I should keep him. I'll tell him you said so. Night, honey. I'll call you tomorrow."

He hit End Call and slumped against Mal again, exhausted. Mal took the phone and held it out to Jeri, who turned her backside toward him. He slid it in and said thank you, and she gave him a wink before going back to work on Damien.

Damien had an IV in and was apparently stoned and sleeping, and Mal was actually a little jealous of his friend.

"What'd she say?" He ran his hands—clean for the first time in days—through Tevyn's snarled hair, smoothing the curls the best he could.

"She said you were a good man and she's so glad we're together now. Mallory, she doesn't even know what day it is, and she knew that. Isn't that weird?"

"I'm glad someone approves," he said.

"Yeah, well, me too."

Mal was warm and safe, and his stomach was at least sated for the first time in a week. He leaned against the comfortable seat and pulled Tevyn closer and let his eyes drift shut. So many grown-up things to attend to—but they had this moment, right here.

It was like coming down the mountain. They were alive. They were together. It was all he could ask.

## Feet on the Ground

**TEVYN** tried really hard to hold on to his patience.

He'd thought he could deal with Charlie's protectiveness, but he hadn't realized how bad it would get.

She'd sailed into their hospital room, past guards and reporters, by dint of chutzpah alone. Once there, she'd pretty much thrown a bag of clothes at Tevyn and gone to slobber all over Mallory without giving Tev so much as a second glance.

"Oh my God! Lookit you! You've lost twenty pounds, you bastard!"

"I skipped dessert for a week." Mallory looked over at Tevyn and winked. "You want to change first?" he asked.

Before their night of fluids and tests, they'd both been given a thorough look-over for parasites but had begged to use the shower cubicles instead of getting a sponge bath. Blissful hot water—Tevyn wasn't sure about Mallory, but he'd spent a good long time soaping everything six times and scrubbing his teeth until his enamel was at risk. It had been good to get clean the night before, but it would be even better to get out of the hospital gown.

They'd both asked for their sweaters back. Everything else could be burned, but there was no denying that those sweaters had saved their lives. They sat, neatly folded, in a plastic bag with their wallets, which had been recovered at the crash site.

"Yeah." Tevyn scowled at Charlie, who smiled back with teeth that looked pointed. "I was hoping to change right here."

"Oh, sweetie, there's a bathroom right there. Didn't you see it?"

Tevyn rolled his eyes so hard he had to reclaim them from the back of his head. "Just didn't think I'd need it." And with that he dropped his hospital gown off his shoulders and stood naked while he rooted through the department store bag.

"*Deadpool* boxer briefs," he said blankly.

"They were on sale."

"Wranglers." That wasn't so bad. Only so many ways you could screw up jeans.

"Like my nephew wears," she said, all sweetness.

"A Shaun White T-shirt."

"He's in your profession, right?"

"And a hooded sweatshirt with Batman on it."

"That *is* age appropriate, isn't it?"

Tevyn looked at Mallory for help and saw that the entire wardrobe conversation had sailed right over his head.

He was staring at Tevyn's body—underfed and stringy after the last week—with a sort of wistful hunger.

Tevyn caught his eyes and smiled wolfishly.

Mallory licked his lips.

Without a damn given to Charlie, Tevyn dropped the paper underwear the hospital had provided and pulled the damned *Deadpool* underwear on without a second thought. Keeping eye contact with Mallory, he put on the Shaun White T-shirt and the Batman hooded sweatshirt and the plain white gym socks, Wranglers, and high-top Converse tennis shoes like this was how he wanted Mallory to see him. When he was done, he walked to the side of Mallory's bed—in front of Charlie—and leaned over to take his mouth in the kiss that had been brewing between them from the moment he'd seen that wistful hunger.

Mallory returned it, sweetly, and Charlie, who had been in full cry the entire time, shut up like a switch had been clicked.

Tevyn pulled back and stared at Mallory, surprised. "I didn't know we could do that here," he said.

"The hospital?"

He was getting used to that little quirk in Mallory's lips that indicated he was kidding.

"Off the mountain. On the mountain, that was easy. I was wondering if we could do that here."

"No frostbite," Mallory said, winking. He rubbed the dark beard that had grown on his narrow face in the last week. "But I may want to shave when we get to the hotel."

Tevyn rubbed his own blond scruff—not hardly enough to call stubble. "Me too, unless you like the style."

Mallory's hand cupping the back of his head was a welcome surprise, and this kiss packed some heat.

And that's where they were when Charlie got up and let the reporters in.

**WHAT** followed was a miserable media circus of cell phones pushed into his face as every blogger on the planet tried to make him a hero and Mal and Damien into grateful acolytes at the altar of his awesomeness.

"What made you decide to bring Mr. Ward and Mr. Armstrong down the mountain with you, Tevyn? It must have been a hard decision, knowing you could have made it so much faster yourself."

"Do you think I could have done that without Mallory's help?" he'd asked, growing angry. "Do you think either of us could have brought Damien down alone? Even Damien helped—and not just by being positive either. He kept the fire going when we were both exhausted. Do you know how important that was? It's the only reason we're not psychotic or dead! Mal spent an hour in a blizzard bringing in firewood so we could tend to Damien's leg! He risked his life so the three of us could make it down together. You all see the medals and the pro-athlete thing and think I'm a hero, but on that mountain, it had to be all of us or none of us, and the blizzard didn't give a *damn* about my trophies. Now get the hell out. We're fucking *tired*!"

*That* was what made Mallory kick them all out— while still wearing his hospital gown. He shoved the door closed and turned to glare at his business partner.

"That was really awful," he said. "What's gotten into you?"

Charlie glared back mutinously. "That's going to be your life now, do you realize that?"

"Not really," Tevyn muttered, grabbing the suitcase with Mallory's clothes. He pulled out boxer briefs, a pair of jeans, a T-shirt, and a zip-up hoodie. "They were sort of rabid today. I assume coming down the damned mountain after a week got them riled." He glared at Charlie too. "What is your problem with me, by the way? This didn't used to be so bad!"

"You could hurt him!" she snarled.

"Charlie," Mallory said kindly, "that's really between Tev and—"

"Mallory, go change," Tevyn said, keeping his eyes locked with Charlie's. "In the bathroom. Please. Me and Charlie have to have a talk before we get to the hotel."

Mallory looked from one to the other, and then, God love him, bailed.

"You're too young for him," Charlie said as soon as he'd disappeared.

"He thought that too."

"You sleep with anything that moves."

"Not anymore."

"He's—"

"Kind?" Tevyn said, and she blinked. "Strong? Funny? Vulnerable? Do you think I don't know that? How about smart? Did you factor that in? He knows who I am, and he knows who he is, and we're both ready to be us together."

"Did you notice all those reporters?" she demanded. "Did you see what happened there?"

Tevyn sighed. Of course he had. Tevyn had been the hero—everyone else had been his accessory. "Do you think I give a *damn* about that?" he returned. "And

I know Mallory doesn't. Do you know why he comes to our sporting events? Not just mine. He comes to all his clients', even if not as much."

"To make sure everyone is doing well in the season," she said, like she was reciting company policy. She might have been. "To see that the client's needs are being met and to adjust for any flux in the income stream."

"To hear our names over the intercom and know he helped make our dreams come true," Tevyn told her.

She gasped and covered her mouth. "That's not—"

"Company policy? Maybe not. But it's why *he's* there. Because he doesn't want to be the superstar. He wants to help the superstar do his job. Well, he can help me do my job by holding my fucking hand." Tevyn closed his eyes. They were getting the first flight out of town as soon as they knew Damien would recover. Mallory promised to be there. "He can help me live my life by being by my side. Is that what you wanted to hear?"

"No," she said, her voice wobbling. "Because it sounds reasonable. It sounds like you're going to be his happy ever after, his knight in shining armor. But I'm all he's got, do you understand me? If his knight in shining armor breaks his heart, I might not be able to pick up the pieces!"

"Then work with me here!" Tevyn begged. "Maybe if I *am* his knight in shining armor, you don't have to be taking care of him all alone."

She looked at his suitcase then and pulled fitfully at the zipper. "If you make him move to Colorado, I'll gut you in your sleep," she said, and Tevyn swallowed nervously, because she meant that.

"Only for a month or two in the summer," he said. "So we can stay in my grandmother's cabin and let the dog run in the country and play."

"You have a dog?" And oh, thank you Jesus, she sounded hopeful. Like them having a dog meant something to her.

"We plan to get one," he said. "When our lives are settled. He said you'd dogsit."

"It needs to be a big dog." She carefully wiped the eyeliner under her eyes with the edge of her pinky finger. "I'm not letting him go to someone who likes one of those football-sized things that my cat can beat the crap out of."

"Deal." He watched her pull out a pair of loafers for Mal—deck shoes, really, totally impractical in the winter, but they were battered, and he had the feeling they were his favorites and she had known that. "He can't travel with me all the time. I know that. I'd really like someone to help me with his care and feeding," he offered tentatively. "I... we don't have to be at odds."

She turned to him with eyes that were red—but not overflowing. "Hurt him and I will hurt you," she said, and he had no doubt she meant it in every way possible. "You dick around with his heart, kid, and I will never forgive you." At that moment, their doctor came in, and she raised her voice. "Mallory, get your ass in here! I think they're going to spring you, and I'm dying to get the hell out of the hospital!"

Test result after test result was recited, and at the end, Tevyn made the doctor state his HIV status loud and clear. Yeah, sure, he'd been promiscuous, but he'd been *careful*, dammit, and it was important for Mallory to know that.

Mallory was special. What they were going to do together was special.

"So we can go?" Mallory asked after the final instruction to take their vitamins and report anything out of the ordinary.

"You may certainly go," the doctor agreed.

"Do we know how our friend is? Mr. Ward?"

Dr. Brekken sobered. "He is in his second round of surgery right now," he said quietly. "After recovery, he'll spend a couple of days in the ICU. I wouldn't count on visiting him until at least tomorrow."

Tevyn closed his eyes.

"Understood," Mallory replied. Tevyn felt a tug at his hand, and Mal was there, lacing their fingers while towing his suitcase behind him. "I'll see you tomorrow."

They went walking through the hospital, Charlie clicking on her high heels in the lead.

"We'll see him tomorrow," Tevyn said, feeling lost.

"I will," Mallory told him. "You'll be on a plane to Colorado. I'll get the next one out after Damien's stable."

Tevyn must have let out a sound of protest, because Mallory brought their twined hands up so he could kiss Tevyn's knuckles.

"You need to get there," he said softly. "I get it. I get you to myself for tonight. I'll just have to make sure it's some night so it's not our only one."

Tevyn thought about them, together, in a darkened room. "Mal?"

"Yeah?"

"It's not going to be our only one."

"God, I hope not."

"We've waited long enough."

**CHARLIE** had definitely picked a nice hotel—the Hyatt in downtown. They stopped for lunch first, where, per doctor's orders, they stuck to chicken on whole wheat, because their stomachs would be small and sensitive for a little while.

Charlie checked them in and handed Mal the key card, then eyed them both. "I'm the floor below, same room. You know. In case someone needs to sleep in my extra bed."

Tevyn snorted. "I'm not seeing that happening," he said, squeezing Mallory's hand. Just that contact and the whole rest of the world faded away.

They practically ran to their room, and Tevyn sat down to unlace his sneakers while Mallory was still wrestling his suitcase through the door.

Mallory settled the suitcase in the corner of the room and turned to him. "Sore feet?"

Tevyn kicked off the damned shoes and grunted. "Why are you still dressed?"

"Because I'm an old-fashioned sort of guy," Mallory said primly. "I thought, you know, a kiss first?"

Tevyn wanted him naked—all ninety-eight pounds of him at this point, but he wanted it bare, smooth-skinned, knotty-muscled, yielding flesh under his palms.

He came to a halt in front of Mal and reached up to cup his neck. "Fine. Kiss first. C'mere."

Mallory hesitated, and Tevyn could discern the slightest tremble in him. "Don't worry, Mal. I'll treat you real fine."

Mallory closed his eyes—those pretty brown eyes, so sharp and assessing, lively and questing—he closed them and let Tevyn take over.

Tevyn took his mouth first, hard and no bullshit, so Mallory knew he meant business. Then he stroked his neck, his shoulders, ran his hand over his chest through his clothes.

"How warm do you think it is in here?" he murmured in Mallory's ear. "Seventy degrees, you reckon?"

"Practically a sauna," Mal answered, and Tevyn bit his earlobe as a reward.

"Mm…." He let go. "*You* are wearing too many clothes. Take them off."

Mallory's fingers went to the zipper of his hoodie first, and Tevyn helped slide it off his shoulders, where he dropped it on the ground. Mallory Armstrong, who folded all his clothes into little tiny units, let it lie there in a puddle while Tevyn grazed his collarbones with tender lips, laid bare to the edge of his polo shirt.

"Mal?" Tevyn rucked the shirt up and splayed his hand across Mallory's lean stomach.

"Mm? Ah!" The gasp was when Tev went for the nipple, scraping the pad of his thumb across it first.

"I know we've been wearing six layers of clothing, so you might be confused." He pinched the nipple this time, just to hear Mallory whimper. "But this isn't naked."

Mallory fumbled with the hem of his shirt, and Tevyn helped him haul it overhead. Ah! His chest. He had a layer of dark hair down the middle, leading to his happy trail, made more notable by the pale skin. Tevyn closed his mouth over a pink nipple and suckled, welcoming Mal's clenched fingers in his hair. He sucked again, and harder, then scraped his teeth delicately across. Mallory put his hands on Tevyn's shoulders and held on for dear life.

"Knees going," he whispered, and Tevyn pulled away with the intention of leading him to the bed, but Mallory fell to his knees instead, hands on Tevyn's hips, tugging at the Wranglers that were a size too big and needed a belt.

The *Deadpool* underwear went off with the Wranglers, and Tevyn was suddenly, aggressively naked. His cock flopped down, halfway hard and filling, and Mallory moaned.

"Yeah?" Tevyn grabbed his shirts at the shoulder and hauled them over his head, shuddering as Mallory stroked his erection.

"*Tevyn*!" The awe in Mallory's voice was both satisfying and embarrassing.

"More than a growing boy needs, right?" He knew he was large, particularly for someone not tall or bulky.

"It's beautiful." Mallory's breath tickled his head. His tongue, on the other hand, licking across the head, didn't tickle at *all*.

It was Tevyn's turn to close his eyes, to feel the rough silk of Mallory's hair between his fingers. Mallory stroked him with a firm hand and licked with enthusiasm, making happy humming noises in his throat as he explored. He lowered his head slightly and took one of Tevyn's balls in his mouth, carefully, tugging gently before letting it go. Tevyn shuddered and urged him to take the other one, the touch of his lips, his tongue, just right.

His erection ached, and the coil in the pit of his stomach wound painfully tight. He pulled on Mallory's hair until Mallory backed off.

"I want to make love to you," he whispered. "I want to take you in the best way. Come on, Mal. Bed."

He gave Mallory a hand up and steadied him when he overbalanced. "I, uh, need my shaving kit," Mallory mumbled, and even with the lights off, Tevyn could see the blush.

"Go get the lubricant," Tevyn told him, coming up behind Mallory as he stood so he could undo Mal's belt and fly. "But we don't need the rubbers. I know your status, and I made damned sure you know mine."

Mallory paused in the act of fishing something out of his suitcase. "That's... that's monogamy, Tevyn. You know that. That's commitment."

Tevyn shoved at Mallory's pants and boxers, humming as bare skin was exposed. "Yeah, I know."

Mallory didn't move—seemed, in fact, to be catching his breath—until Tevyn wrapped his arms around Mallory's waist and ground his nakedness up against Mal's bare backside. "I don't want anything less. You?"

Mallory turned and fumbled for his hand, pushing the small bottle into it. At least the thing was full. "No. You know... making sure."

Tevyn kissed him again, tasting the salt of his own precum. The stakes were higher now because Mallory's mouth had been on him, had taken him in. Mallory was already his. He just didn't feel it yet.

"C'mon, Mal. I'll take really good care of you."

Mallory allowed himself to be kissed backward to the bed, then pulled away to strip the covers down. "I thought it was my job to take care of you," he said wistfully.

"You did," Tevyn told him, sliding into bed. Ah! God! Those nights in his arms, separated by the clothing, the fear—this was Mallory's skin all over his, and he gloried in it, wanting to scent mark Mallory's body like a cat. "You took care of us every day. You kept us talking, kept us happy. You tended the fire, made Damien laugh. You put one foot in front of the other when I know you didn't have a damned thing left in you, because you knew we wouldn't leave you behind. You've taken care of me and my grandmother for five years, when I was too young and too stupid to know how to make you mine. It's my turn, Mallory Armstrong. It's my turn to take care of you. It's my turn to show you I can make you mine."

He rolled then, on top of Mallory's long, lean body, because he knew Mal could bear his weight. He started out kissing his mouth but didn't stay there long. Mallory's jaw, his neck, his collarbone, he nipped and nuzzled each place, knowing his short beard and sharp love bites would leave marks, and not caring. Mallory's noises got louder, more frequent, more desperate as Tevyn went, and Tevyn let him.

There was nobody here but the two of them. Mallory could scream obscenities, could sob, could come, and it would be just them, their bare bodies, and this bed.

Tevyn sucked his nipples again, harder, leaving marks on his chest, downward. He sucked on the soft skin of Mallory's concave stomach, ignoring Mal's breathless protests because most of them boiled down to "Oh God, please!"

Tevyn pleased very much to give Mallory Armstrong pleasure.

When he got to Mallory's straining, dripping erection, Tevyn pleased very much indeed.

"Lookit you," he whispered, before taking it into his mouth. Mallory was very long, if not as thick as Tevyn. Tevyn would ride it someday, sliding down its length until he straddled Mal completely, and the thought made him tingle everywhere, in particular his entrance. He had no problem being penetrated, but damn.

With Mallory, he wanted to do the owning.

People all over the world wanted a piece of Tevyn Moore, wanted to have a claim to a part of him—his logo, his talent, his body. But only Mallory had ever cared for him, taken care *of* him, and Tevyn wanted Mallory all to himself.

Mallory's wordless cries had settled into a long moan of arousal, and as Tevyn took him to the back of his throat, he swallowed the moan and tried words again. "Tev, gonna come—too soon—"

Tevyn pulled back and stroked him, hard and sure. "You think this thing is over when you come?" he asked, spitting on two fingers of his free hand. "You think I won't take you, fuck you, pound you into the mattress because you had one orgasm?"

Mallory made a strangled sound between a laugh and a groan and a gasp. "I am so loud!" he complained.

"Yeah," Tevyn said, licking the head of Mallory's dick just to hear him make more noise. "And every sound you make is 'Tevyn, do me more. Do me harder. Do me until I scream.'" He deep-throated again to feel the head against his throat, to feel the veins under his lips as he pulled back, to hear the glorious sound— between a grunt and a groan—that Mallory emitted when he did.

He did it again, but this time he fingered Mallory's entrance and was delighted when Mallory sucked in a breath and held it.

"Mal?" he whispered, wiggling his finger, stretching at that tight ring of muscle until Mallory quivered.

"Wha?"

"You have to breathe. You have to relax. This won't hurt if you relax."

"But… oh… I'm not sure… oh my God… oh… *oh*!"

Tevyn kept stretching—and kept sucking Mallory's hard cock as well. Every wiggle of his fingers amped Mallory up a notch, every swipe of his tongue pulled his string tighter.

But he was clenching, and that was no good either.

"Push," he whispered. "Push against me. Push— whoa! Yes!" Both fingers slid in to the hilt just as he bottomed out with Mallory's cock, swallowing against it in the back of his throat. Mallory's erection wept, bitter and salty, into his mouth, and the taste was the only drug Tevyn had ever craved.

Mallory gave a short, hot spurt into Tevyn's mouth, and Tevyn scissored his fingers.

And that did it. Mallory shouted—actually shouted— pouring his orgasm into Tevyn's throat as Tevyn swallowed happily.

His. Mallory was his.

"Oh…," Mallory breathed, going limp. His clench around Tevyn's fingers softened, and Tevyn figured he was about ready. He reached for the lubricant next to Mal's hip and dumped some on his fingers, then spread it around Mallory's despoiled entrance and stretched him some more.

Mallory's next noise was curious—and aroused.

"I want to be inside you, Mal. Please tell me you want that too."

Mallory looked stoned—stoned and sleepy, his eyes at half-mast, his body sprawled beyond his control. But at Tevyn's words, his eyes snapped open and his mouth parted ever so slightly.

"Yeah, Tevyn. Please. I need you inside me so bad."

Tevyn squirted some more slick and oiled his cock with it before pushing himself up the bed. "Spread your legs, baby, bent at the knees. That's right. I want to see your face here. I need to see you love me."

He hadn't meant to say that—oh God. The words. The big scary words that could ruin any sex. But Mallory was a man, and men didn't run away.

"Of course I love you," Mallory said in wonder. "Of course I do… oh… oh yes."

Tevyn pushed forward, slowly, waiting for Mallory to expand around him. He did, his body growing more lax, more accommodating with every millimeter. Tevyn's head popped in and Mallory let out a low "Whooa!" which acted as encouragement. Slowly, waiting to see if it was okay, Tevyn claimed his lover's body, felt his heat take over their joining, warmed himself in the glory of Mallory Armstrong's sex.

Finally he was seated completely, kissing Mallory's sweaty forehead, breathing softly on his temple. "You good?"

"I've never… oh yes. Yes, it's good. It's so good. Move? Move, Tev. I really need you to—yes!"

Never done this before? Yes, he'd said as much, but he was made for this. Tevyn started to thrust, in and out, the timeless dance of the male body. Mallory's ass clenched so tightly around him that it felt like a fist, a beautiful milking fist, taking everything Tevyn was made to give.

He kept thrusting, listening to the music of Mallory's desire grow steadily louder, more breathless. Mallory clung to his shoulders, to his biceps, his brown eyes big and surprised, his pupils blown with passion, his face open and vulnerable, showing every moment of pleasure, every moment of doubt.

Tevyn kept fucking until the doubt was scoured from his heart, until the pleasure took control of him, opened him up for Tevyn's plunder.

His eyes went to half-mast then, his mouth opened slackly, and the steadily rising pleasure noises became all one sound.

"Yes," Mallory begged. "Yes. Yes. Yes. Yes."

Tevyn shuddered and picked up his pace, angling himself so he'd pass... right... *there* with every thrust, that place right there, that made Mal's hands tighten on his shoulders, that made his voice deepen.

"Oh my God, Tevyn—*yes!*"

Again and again and again—oh hells, Tevyn wanted to do this forever, wanted this steadily escalating searing pleasure to ride his synapses until there was nothing else but Tevyn buried inside his lover, not cock in ass, but heart in heart.

But bodies are fallible, need release, and Tevyn's orgasm was sweeping up his spine, inevitable, glorious.

"You ready?" he asked Mallory. "You ready? I'm going to come. Inside you, Mal. Forever and ever."

Mal let out a low groan, and his arms went limp as every other muscle convulsed. Oh wow—Tevyn could feel him spurting again, hot and slick between them, not even a hand on his erection as Tevyn rose to his own peak.

"So good," Mallory whispered, spent. He raised his hands to Tevyn's chest and pinched his nipples, and that was all Tevyn needed, a little encouragement, a little extra bite.

He went pitching off the climax cliff with a turbo burst of desire, burying his face against Mal's throat and roaring in release.

Mallory cried out again and Tevyn bit his shoulder—hard—as his orgasm rocked his body, his heart, the foundations of his world.

When he came to, he was still buried in Mallory's ass, and Mallory's arms were up around his shoulders, holding him tight.

Comforting him, maybe, comforting them both, because that thing they had just done was bigger than sex, mightier. If Tevyn hadn't wanted it so bad, hadn't committed to making Mallory his from the very beginning, it might even have been terrifying.

As it was, he licked the bruised spot on Mallory's shoulder, being tender now that the mark was there.

"Love you, Mallory. Love you so much."

"Love you back," Mallory whispered. "I'm... I'm lost."

Tevyn moved a little, fucking him some more even as his spent member grew smaller.

"I'm here. Inside you. Every day. Remember that, when we have to be apart, okay?"

"Yeah."

"Promise me." Tevyn pulled back and made sure Mallory could see his eyes. "You have to promise me that I'll be inside you, in your heart, all the time."

Mallory searched his face, seeing far too much, probably, about what Tevyn didn't want to admit. "You'll always be inside me, Tev. You haven't left. Not in five years. You think I'll ever forget you after this?"

"Good," Tevyn growled, taking his mouth.

Mallory gave back, because that's what he did.

Tevyn could only hope he'd given enough.

# *A Thousand Miles*

**MALLORY** usually woke up all together, in one whole piece. At home, he rolled out of bed and went straight to the bathroom to brush his teeth, take his shower, and begin his day.

He woke up in the darkened hotel room slowly, trying to put things together in his head, but not everything fit.

Except maybe Tevyn's body, lodged solidly in Mallory's own.

They'd fallen asleep that way after their third—fourth?—time making love.

Mallory was covered in come. Down his backside, his thighs, his stomach, his chest, his mouth.

Eyes still closed, Tevyn at his back, inside him and filling slowly, Mal remembered that glorious, surprising moment when he'd been sucking Tevyn's cock and Tev had come—effortlessly, body arching in complete abandon.

Complete trust.

Tevyn started to pump, in and out, and Mallory gasped. "Again?"

"Say what you really want," Tevyn whispered, reaching around to fondle his stiffening erection.

Mallory could because Tevyn would give him what he wanted, every time. "Please," Mallory moaned, needing him again, again, again....

Tevyn's slow, sensual pump inside him continued, his body stretched, exhausted, but responding anyway. "Sore?" Tevyn asked, being considerate like he had been all night.

"No," Mallory lied. He'd lied the last time too. Tevyn was larger than life in every area—particularly the one moving in one of Mallory's tenderest places. But Mallory had waited so long, needed so badly. He'd lie as many times as he had to, as long as this dreamy ache continued, this haze of stretching, of pleasure so acute it passed the border to pain.

Tevyn's lips at the back of his neck tickled deliciously. "Good."

His thrusts continued, his cock growing harder and bigger as he woke up too. With a little shove at Mallory's shoulder, Tevyn pushed him from lying on his side to sprawling facedown on the mattress, legs splayed as Tevyn took over his body one more time.

He was so sensitized, so sensitive, by this point, that the pressure of his abdomen against the mattress was enough to pleasure his own erection, and he lay there, drowsy, lost in the dreamy sensation of being taken so often his body was comfortable with being used.

He heard his own sex noises, vibrating against the mattress, and couldn't seem to stop. He had no control anymore. Tevyn had taken control the first time he'd taken Mallory and had never given it back. Mallory was at his mercy, and Tevyn was kind, and considerate, and gentle—but when it came to letting Mallory get away with just lying there and taking it, he was anything but merciful.

Responding to Tevyn's touch was Mallory's mission.

Tevyn pulled out and Mallory actually whimpered at the loss.

"Hands and knees, Mal," Tevyn ordered softly, and Mallory went, beyond being vulnerable and on display. Tevyn's hands, callused, tender, along his back, his flanks, his thighs, his backside, sent a quiver through his core, and he rocked backward, toward Tevyn's groin, begging without words.

Tevyn didn't let him down.

His glide into Mallory's body was so welcome Mallory almost wept with the completeness of it. The next few moments were a long, slow power-fuck, and Mallory couldn't have stopped the noises coming from his throat if his life had been at stake. He needed this. He needed every second, every millimeter, every thrust.

The orgasm washing up from his balls was a surprise only because he would have thought he'd been wrung dry by now. Not quite. Slow, painful, it racked his entire body, spilling hot and salty in a chafing spurt.

Tevyn gave a holler behind him and collapsed, sweaty, the cloak Mallory had worn on his back for most of the night.

As he sprawled on the bed, facedown, Tevyn kissing his back and neck, his phone buzzed into the silence.

"God," Tevyn moaned. "Already?"

Mallory half laughed. "It's nine," he said softly. "Time to get ready."

"No."

Mallory wriggled, dislodging Tevyn and then rolling over to kiss him messily, morning dick breath and all.

"Yes," he said. "C'mon, baby. You know you need to go."

The night before, sometime between round two and round three, Charlie had called and asked them if they wanted to go out to dinner or if they were staying in for room service. Mallory had already been looking at the menu.

Then she'd told them that Tevyn's flight left at 11:30 a.m., and Lyft would be there at 9:30. Mallory had set his (brand-new and awkward) phone for nine at the time, thinking it was unnecessary. He was an early riser. Tevyn was too—why would they need an alarm?

He hadn't counted on round three, four, or, just now, five.

"Of course I need to go," Tevyn groused, sounding younger than Mal for the first time since… since the night he'd asked Mallory to stay. "I…." He ran his fingertips lightly through Mallory's sweaty beard. "I want to see what you look like again after you shave this," he said with a wink.

"I'll send you a picture—shit."

Tevyn chuckled. "Don't have a phone yet. I may have to buy one at the damned airport."

"Dammit. You take mine. I'll get my own today. I'll have time after we visit the hospital. Charlie and I might have time to drive home if Damien's stable, and I'll catch a flight from San Francisco." It was a bigger airport; the odds of getting a flight were much better.

"So I'll have all your settings?" Tevyn teased. He knew as well as Mallory that about all Mal had time to do was add Charlie to his contact list. He'd planned to import her contacts later that day—hopefully after they saw that Damien was going to be all okay and they were driving home to his apartment.

"Yup. Charlie. And, you know." He sobered. "Me."

"You're the only one I need," Tevyn said, grim and shiny-eyed. "I don't want to go without you."

Mallory swallowed. "I don't want to let you go. But Missy needs to see a familiar face."

"And Damien deserves to have one of us there."

And that was the hell of it and the absolute truth.

"If you begged me to stay, I would," Tevyn said, and Mallory's eyes burned. He'd thought he'd been vulnerable splayed out for Tevyn's pleasure. That was nothing to what Tevyn had just given him.

"But I love you," Mallory rasped. "So I won't. Because I'm going to trust this isn't the end. That nothing will stop us from finding a way."

Tevyn nodded and dashed the back of his hand over his eyes. "I'm being silly," he confessed. "I—I fell

in love with you because you would always be there
when I needed you."

"And I fell in love with you because you would
always be strong enough to do what needed to be done."

They kissed, one more time, and Tevyn rolled
away to shower.

Mallory joined him, their hands on each other
sensual but not sexual. This was simply a way to not let
go for another ten minutes, that was all. Tevyn didn't
have a bag to pack, even—all he had was another pair
of those dreadful underwear to put on clean. Tevyn
had time to watch him shave, staring in wonder as a
leaner, sharper version of Mallory's face emerged from
the dark, week-old beard he'd grown in the wilderness.
When he was done Tevyn caressed his soft, newly
exposed skin, then stepped back and took a quick
picture.

Mal gasped, embarrassed. He was wearing a towel
and nothing else. "Tevyn!"

"Mine," Tevyn said simply. "I want to show people
I've got someone. 'Who?' they'll say. 'This guy. He'll
take care of me.'"

Mallory cupped the back of his head and pulled
him forward in his own claiming kiss. "I will."

"He'll make my dreams come true."

Because that's what Mallory had tried to do from
the very beginning.

"With every breath," Mallory vowed.

"Good. I'll see you in a few. Text me when you
have a new number."

One more kiss, and he was gone.

Charlie was uncharacteristically silent as she
piloted her Element through Sacramento traffic to the

Med Center. "These people have no idea how easy they have it," she muttered. "If I was trying to find a parking spot in San Francisco, I'd have to bring a goat, a knife, and a sacred object."

"I think in Sacramento they settle for an IPA and some artisan bread," Mallory bantered back, and Charlie laughed shortly.

"How are you?"

What was he going to say? Sore? Heart sore? Irritated at the gods of time, space, and mortality?

"Tired."

"Yeah, that much I gathered. I gotta say, I'm liking you without the beard. Tevyn could wear it—sort of that beatnik-surfer-kid thing he's got going. You, not so much."

"He didn't shave this morning—I think he agrees."

She grunted and took a turn into the gleaming white multilevel parking garage boasted by the Med Center. "So. Am I getting any details today?"

"Did you get any with Keith?" he countered, not sure he was ready to spill so soon after Tevyn had been inside of him.

"Occasionally. For example, you once told me he was one and done and blowjobs every other Thursdays."

"I was drunk!" Oh God. Mallory needed to warn Tevyn not to let him drink, ever.

"Do you lie when you're drunk?" she asked, like she didn't know the answer to that.

"No." He went home with porn stars and got loud in bed—but apparently he got loud in bed anyway, so maybe it was just the porn model that came with the alcohol. Either way, he didn't lie. As he'd told Tevyn, his sex life with Keith had been pleasant.

What had happened the night before—and this morning—had not been "pleasant." It had been earth-shattering, pleasure-to-pain uncomfortable, and glorious.

"So tell me the truth now," Charlie said, her lips twisting as she found them a parking spot on the fourth floor. "How was last night?"

"I hit the octave above high C," Mallory said with a completely straight face. "I'm pretty sure the people next to us called the front desk for another room—and those walls aren't thin."

Charlie parked the car and burst out laughing, so loudly and so hysterically, Mallory checked twice to make sure she'd turned off the ignition and wasn't a danger to anyone nearby.

"What?" he asked. "You wanted the truth!"

"I don't know… I sort of wish it had been a bust!" she told him. "I wish he'd been a selfish punk in bed, so I could say 'I told you so' and you wouldn't have to move to Colorado for the summers!"

*Aw. Charlie.*

"We need to fix the cabin up first," he said, like the idea of visiting in Colorado for the summer, in that little cabin at the base of a ski resort mountain, didn't make him insanely happy. "But I'm not giving up Mom's house on the peninsula. I finally got everything painted the way I like it. He's a wanderer, Charlie. Anywhere I make my home, he'll come wandering back."

She cocked her head. "You're awfully confident. That's not like you at all."

Mallory smiled a little, not sure if he could explain. "He asked me to stay with him. The night before the crash. And I stayed with him to calm him down, because Missy was dying and he was hurting. And the next day the world exploded, and I said, 'You should go down the mountain without us,' and you know what he said?"

"You told him what?" she asked, visibly upset.

"I said he should go bring help. And he refused. He said it was all of us or none of us. And he looked me dead in the eye and said, 'You promised you'd stay.' Because that meant something to him. Because he'd been in love with me all along, but he didn't believe I'd be there for him until we got down that mountain together. So yeah, I believe in him, Charlie. He believed in me, and it got me down the mountain alive. I believe in him right back, and it's going to get us through the next couple of weeks, and it's going to get us through our crazy schedules and his career. I *believe*, dammit. You should too."

"Why would you do that?" she asked, obviously back at the first thing he'd said. "Why would you tell him to go down without you?"

Mallory grimaced. "Because he had a better chance at survival. I… I didn't want to think of a world without him."

She scrubbed at her eyes. "I am so mad at you right now I can't even…. Go. Go say hi to Damien. Go make sure he's okay. I'll be out here trying to find words for exactly why—"

He kissed her cheek. "You're mad because you almost lost me, sweetheart. And I would have felt awful about leaving you. But I didn't. So maybe stop obsessing about how my love life is screwing with your perception of reality and remember why you love me in the first place."

"Because you can say things like that with a straight face," she said sourly. "Fine. By the way, can I say giving him your phone was both chivalrous and impossibly dumb?"

"We're getting another one today, right?"

She grunted and looked at her own phone, which was buzzing quietly. "Yeah. But he just told me he was boarding the plane and he wants me to tell you he loves you. *That's* what's dumb, because I haven't been this girl since high school."

Mallory winked at her. "Your taste in shoes is way better than it was in high school." When they'd met in college, she'd been all combat boots and plaid shirts. Now she was all Louboutin and Jimmy Choo.

"Should I tell him you love him too?" she asked with acid in her voice.

"Tell him safe travels, and I'll be there as soon as I can," Mallory told her mildly. "He'll know it's me that way."

She sighed. "You're impossible, you know that? You used to do that to me in college. 'Yeah, I signed up for this super hard business course that everybody's afraid of but it looks challenging. Do it with me, it'll be fun!'"

"And it was," Mallory said, heading for the skybridge that took them to the ICU.

"Yeah, but there I was, hyperventilating, and you just kept smiling. 'Yeah, look, they've got an office in the superbig skyscraper with a helicopter pad—let's lease it!' And you'd done all the math and we could afford it, but I was still hyperventilating and you were like, 'Makes total sense!' Remember?"

"That was only six years ago, Charlie. I'm not senile."

"But you do that!" she complained, following him. "You look at these things that everyone else thinks are impossible, and you've done the math and the logic, and you... you...."

"Sled down the hill on an airplane wing behind the one guy on the planet who could actually steer the damned thing without killing us all?"

"Click," she said, her perfectly made-up eyes widening. "And it all makes sense."

He smiled and kept walking.

"You know," she said, keeping up in high heels, because Charlie could. "You might want to tell him about how you do that."

"Do what?" he asked, all innocence.

"Never mind. You know? Never mind. By now, he probably already knows."

Their banter faded then, because they had entered the ICU. Charlie had texted, and they followed the directions to Damien's room, arriving in time to see Preston emerge from the sliding glass door and dart away from them to the other end of the hallway.

"That doesn't bode well," Charlie murmured.

"That's Preston."

"Oh, he's the one who always had the service dog with him." Charlie's voice dropped. "Anxiety?"

"I think he doesn't do well with people." Mallory thought there might be more to it than that, but Preston was smart—he'd helped his brother draw up the business plan—and intuitive. Glen and

Damien couldn't say enough good things about him, and if he was shy around strangers, well, who wasn't? Mallory's job was to accept people for what they could do and not be mad at them for what they couldn't.

They slid into the room Preston had vacated and saw Glen, scowling at an awake Damien and muttering to himself.

"Bad time?" Mallory asked, going to the bedside to shake Damien's hand.

Damien squeezed his tight and smiled. He looked better and awful at the same time.

"How's it going?" Mallory asked because obviously *something* was going on.

"Well, they saved the leg," Damien said, sounding vastly relieved.

"Which is great and all," Glen muttered, "but it wasn't like he wouldn't be part of the company without it."

Mallory thought about the controls of the helicopter. "Aren't they all hand controls? I mean, it's not like you step on the gas or hit the brake, right?"

Damien scowled. "I don't want to be a burden, like I was on the mountain—"

Mallory scowled back. "We couldn't have done what we did without you, you know that, right? It had to be three of us or none of us."

"You had to drag my ass down—"

"And what if we did?" Mal snapped. "If it had been me, would you have just left me in the shelter with a batch of firewood and hoped for the best?"

"No!" Damien rasped. "But I'm the one who crashed the stupid helicopter in the first place. You and Tevyn didn't say one damned thing about it, but—"

"But your intel said thirty knots!" Glen shouted, and they all winced, because raised voices in the ICU weren't cool. "You were told it was safe, then those winds spiked out of nowhere. I looked at the weather patterns, Damien—I was trying to figure out where the hell you were, remember? Everything we had said you took off in thirty knots, and it should have been choppy but doable. You followed your flight plan. A rush of wind through that damned canyon spiked up and knocked you on your ass. You can't plan for shit like that! And you can't blame yourself, and you can't feel crappy because you got hurt."

"Preston won't even look at me," Damien mumbled, and Mallory pinned Glen with a whole other glare.

"Why not?"

Glen looked away. "Because Damien worried him," he said. "Me and Damie are the two people in the world he actually talks to. Losing Damien—that would be like losing a lung for Preston. It… it's hard, when you relate to dogs better than people."

"Damien, he cares about you," Mallory soothed. "You need to calm down and stop stressing your friends out, okay?"

"Where's Tevyn?" he asked fitfully.

"On a plane to Colorado." He had to breathe through that. It was too soon to let him go.

"Why aren't you with him?" Damien demanded, and Mal squeezed his hand again.

"Because our friend was in surgery and we needed to know he was going to be okay before both of us deserted him."

Damien blew out a breath. "Thanks," he mumbled. "I… I'm being a whiny asshole. But thank you. I know how much you want to be with him right now."

"Well, we dragged you down a mountain, Damien. Can't just leave you now."

Damien let go of his hand and waved him to a chair. "Sit. I need to give you pointers for how to deal with the press."

Mallory smiled with all teeth. "You have pointers for that?"

"Yeah. They start with making sure the back of your gown is tied. The whole world got a load of your backside when you stepped in front of Tevyn and started shooing people out of the room."

Mallory's eyes went wide, and Charlie let out a choked guffaw. "How'd my ass look?" he asked numbly.

"Scrawny. Tell me you've eaten since then."

"Two whole times. Skipped breakfast. Felt self-indulgent." The truth was, he hadn't even been hungry.

Damien scowled. "Yeah. I'm still on IV fluids." His eyes fluttered closed for a moment, and then he opened them. "I've got one more surgery," he said. "This afternoon. Stay till tomorrow, okay? I…." He looked at Glen. "I'd love to see Preston too."

Glen nodded. "I'll make sure he knows. Sleep, man. I'll keep Mal company."

Damien's eyes shut for what looked like real sleep, and Mallory sighed and looked at Charlie.

"You can go home," he said. "I'll get on the plane from here instead."

She grunted. "I'd stay here, Mal, but…."

"But we sort of have a business to run," he muttered. "You know what the only thing I actually brought with me to Donner Summit was, right?"

"Your laptop? Yeah, I know. I gave Glen your IP address so he could try to track you, but, you know…."

"It all slid off the mountain with the chopper. Yeah. Tell you what. If you go get me a laptop and a phone, I'll stay here with Glen and set everything up."

Charlie grunted. "Fine. I liked my plan of going into the city better, but fine. I'll water your plants again— they survived last week, they can survive now."

"Thanks, sweetheart."

She stood and kissed his cheek. "An excuse to go shopping. I should thank you. K Street, right?"

"Yup," Glen told her. "And if Mallory's going to stay, I could use a lift there and back. Damien's going to want some of his own clothes too. Tevyn's go bag was the right choice to save, but all Damie's clothes are back in his apartment in Burlingame."

They left, and Mallory sank into the overstuffed chair. The ICU was a scary place—tubes and machines and quietly efficient hospital personnel. But they'd done their best to make visitors comfortable, and that was kind.

He tilted his head back and closed his eyes, remembering the look on Tevyn's face that morning, after their last kiss, when his eyes were still closed and he was smiling.

"Mal?"

Mallory opened his eyes and smiled gently. "Hi, Preston."

"Is the girl gone?"

"Yeah." Preston didn't like strangers—and someone like Charlie, assertive and brash, would terrify him. "She's gone. Come sit for a while."

"Thanks."

Preston really was beautiful—but he wasn't great on eye contact. It wasn't until he'd sat down, spine rigid against the overstuffed seat, that Mallory really felt he'd stay.

"Hospitals stink like piss," he said loudly, then winced. "Sorry, Mallory. I try not to do that. Blurt shit out."

"It's okay. I don't think Damien would mind."

"That was a bad seven days," he said, seemingly out of left field. "I hated being afraid."

"He missed you." So much.

Preston actually risked a look at him. "Missed me how?"

"Missed you a lot. Like you were someone special to him." This was thin territory for Preston. Mallory had once asked him why he liked handling dogs so much, and he'd gone on for an hour about his favorite dog—Preacher—and had never answered the question.

"Damien is special," he said miserably. "I wanted Preach and Scarlet to find him so bad."

"Well, we found you, and that was okay too."

Preston made a near miss with Mallory's eyes and let out a small smile with a little tic in his cheek. "Yes, you did. You were lucky you didn't swerve into the road. Tevyn must be very good on a snowboard."

"He's a genius," Mallory said. "Like you are with dogs." He remembered his and Tevyn's plans then and thought that he might have a topic Preston wouldn't mind discussing. "That reminds me, we want to get a dog."

"What kind?"

"Well, any kind, really—a mixed breed is probably best. Something big that likes snow and doesn't mind traveling. Something calm in crowds that likes to run."

Preston smiled slowly. "I have a friend whose bitch is whelping—she's real sweet. She had Scarlet, and she and Preacher are my favorites, but Preacher's getting old." His head drooped. "Preacher's getting old. I might need one of those dogs to train myself. Do you want me to train it?" He perked up again, like this was the thing he'd been waiting for.

"Simple stuff?" Mallory said, because it would be great if the poor creature could not poop in a helicopter. "Potty training, get the stick, crate training I guess."

Preston nodded, such complete contentment on his face Mallory wished he'd asked for a dog three years ago, when Damien and Glen had first brought him the proposition for Gecko Inc.

"I can do something for you," he said. "I felt bad—you gave us our dream, and I couldn't do anything for you. And then I wanted to find Damien, but you gave us Damien back instead. And now I can do something for you. That's great."

"You don't have to do anything for us," Mallory told him. "It's great that you want to help people—but sometimes, just being you is enough."

Preston shook his head. "Just being me helps nobody. I need the dogs to be any use at all."

Mallory let out a big sigh. "That's not true," he mumbled. "But I'm too tired to argue right now. Later. I'll argue with you later."

"You can sleep now, until they get back," Preston said. "I'll stay here and watch Damien. I don't mind."

Mallory had no doubt Preston would sit, ramrod straight, watching Damien sleep, until Glen got back. He had no problem with that, really. He kicked off his loafers, curled his legs up on the couch, and let the chill quiet of the ICU take over.

**DAMIEN** made it out of his surgery that afternoon with flying colors. By the morning they were willing to move him out of ICU and into the High Dependency Unit. They estimated he'd be in the hospital for another three or four weeks, and part of that would be learning to walk again. They'd saved the leg, but some seriously infected muscle and bone had to be removed or Damien would have gone into sepsis. He'd need to build up his muscle and learn to compensate for what he'd lost before he could be moved out. And his susceptibility to infection would be incredibly high until the wound made by the broken bones had healed, inside and out.

And of course, the leg was still broken.

Mallory—who had spent the night back in the hotel room, alone, restoring all his electronics and texting Tevyn when he could—promised he'd come back to visit.

"You'd better," Damien had mumbled. "You and Tevyn both. He's not competing again for another two weeks. I expect to have some sort of disgusting visit where you're drooling over each other and weeping. I'll be really disappointed if that doesn't happen."

"Why would they drool?" Preston asked. "They're not dogs, Damie."

"No, but they're bonkers over each other, like dogs are bonkers over bacon. It makes them stupid."

Preston laughed—that was his kind of joke.

Mallory gave Damien a dry look. "That stupidity got you down the damned mountain. Never forget it."

Damien sobered. "I never will. Take care of him, Mallory. He needs you more than I do."

Mallory looked directly at Preston. "And you need him more than you ever needed me," he said.

"Me and the dogs will look after Damien really good when he's better," Preston agreed.

And that was Mallory's cue to leave.

## *Goodbyes and Hellos*

**MISSY** hadn't been a big woman in her prime. Maybe—when she'd been married—she'd topped out at five foot, six inches. But now, in her seventies, after being sick for almost two weeks, she was tiny. Tiny and frail—but still feisty as hell.

Tevyn had walked into the hospital expecting to find her sleepy and quiescent, and had, instead, found her to be the terror of the hospice ward.

"If that woman throws food at my orderlies one more time, I'm going to find a way to slide it in there with a pulley," the head nurse had threatened when she found out whom Tevyn was there to visit.

Tevyn grimaced. Missy had grown up in the mountains—she never had much truck with authority or modern medicine.

"Knock on the door when I'm there," he told the nurse. "I'll bring the food in, and maybe she'll eat a little."

The nurse nodded. "I'll be honest—with her attitude and energy, we were hoping she'd turn things around and walk out of here and prove us all wrong. But she sleeps nearly twenty hours a day, and when we gave her tests for heart disease, we realized it had deteriorated a lot since her last visit. It would be great if her last hours on this earth weren't so troubled, though."

Tevyn nodded emphatically. "It's what I'm here for, ma'am. Sorry about the delay."

The nurse—a stunning, statuesque woman in her fifties with skin the color of dark burnished oak and hair pulled back into a tight bun—gave a slight smile. "You survived a helicopter crash in a blizzard to get here, Mr. Moore. I suspect God saved you from death only so you could provide this woman some comfort as she passed. You're not her only visitor. We understand she's quite a character."

"She's made a baby blanket for every newborn in our church since before I was born," he said proudly. Quilted, knitted, crocheted, or woven—Missy had welcomed every baby into the world with handmade love. "Not one family went hungry on her watch. I don't know who they'll get to watch over the food bank next holiday season. She's the reason it existed."

Nurse Jeffries's smile grew bright. "Then she definitely deserves to see you again. Now if you can convince her to give our orderlies a break, that would be a miracle indeed."

She'd been sleeping when he'd first arrived, tired and a little disoriented from traveling. He sat by her bed and played fitfully with his phone, wishing Mallory would get his so they could communicate.

He'd been dozing for about an hour when he heard her humming, and for a few minutes he lay there, his head on her bed, with his eyes closed, and let the sound wash over him. For a few minutes, he got to pretend he was a kid again, and it was snowing outside, and after she made him hot chocolate and he did his chores, he could go up on the mountain and snowboard down.

He'd started working for the ski resort before he was old enough for a work permit, so he could ride the lifts for free.

Her hand in his hair was comforting—but it let him know it was time to wake up.

"Getting long," she chided, and he yawned and sat up.

"Missed my trim this week," he said, and she laughed. He'd worn it long even in grade school.

"You look scrawny," she said critically. "They not feeding you enough?"

He wasn't sure what the staff had told her while he'd been gone. "Got stranded on a mountain in a blizzard, Grandma. I mean, the snow was great, but the cuisine was for shit."

She cackled and then sobered. "Is that where you were? People kept telling me you'd had mechanical problems, but you were trying to get here. What sort of mechanical problems?"

"Our helicopter crashed in a blizzard and fell off a cliff," he said, not afraid of upsetting her. He was here—she'd want to know why he hadn't been.

"That's a problem!"

"I thought so! So did Mal and Damien."

"Mal was there?" she asked sharply. She always did have a soft spot for Mal. "And who?"

"Damien was our pilot. He was injured in the crash. Mal and I had to bring him down the mountain. It was a thing." He grinned. "There were reporters and everything. You can see Mallory's ass on the internet."

She hissed through her teeth. "That's no way to treat a good man of dignity," she admonished, and he grimaced.

"Yeah. I feel bad about that. He was protecting me." Without any consciousness of himself. Tevyn's heart hurt, leaving him behind.

"He does that." She closed her eyes and settled back into the bed. "Why I had them call him when they knew I wasn't getting up."

Tevyn sighed and slouched in his chair. "It's why we were in the helicopter together," he said. "He didn't want me to do this alone."

"Where is he now?" she asked. Her words were slowing down, more and more breath between them.

"Making sure Damien's okay. He was in a bad way by the time we got down the mountain."

"That must have been rough," she breathed. "Leaving him."

How long would he have to tell her this? "I'm in love with him, Grandma."

She closed her eyes and smiled. "Of course you are. And he loves you back."

That's what he needed to hear. "You okay with that?" They'd never really discussed his sexuality—but he was pretty sure she knew he'd kissed a lot of people in his time.

"He'll treat my baby right," she sighed, and then she was asleep again.

He let out a breath and curled his legs underneath him. Unlike when they were on the mountain, planning to get down, there was nothing to do here during the wait but think about all the things he'd been avoiding in a big way.

**MISSY** woke up again for a little while that night, but she didn't recognize him. She kept asking for his mother, like she was still in school, and he told her a neighbor had her and she'd be fine. Her breathing was more congested than ever—she didn't throw food at the orderlies, but she didn't eat either.

His phone buzzed after that.

*Leaving tomorrow at ten. How you doing?*

Tevyn didn't recognize the number, but there was only one person it could be.

*Tired. Missing you. Missy's in and out. She knew me for a little while.*

*I'm glad. Missing you too. Damien just got out of another surgery. He's a handful.*

*Gah! I hate hospitals! How's Charlie?*

*In San Mateo, watering my plants.*

*Good. She still hate me?*

*No.*

Tevyn actually relaxed a little and realized how much that mattered to him.

*I been thinking.*

*Bout?*

*Everything. Think I'll qualify for the Olympics next year?*

*Yes.*

He laughed. Of course Mallory would think that.

*Maybe after that I should cut down on competition. I was going to teach snowboarding, but maybe I want to do more.*

*Like?*

Now *that* was the question, wasn't it? *I've got no idea. It's just, we almost died.*

*I was there.*

*And I saw then that you were the thing I wanted most. Not my next competition. I still want to compete, but if I can have you too, think of all the things we can do.*

*I'm all for surfing. Someplace WARM.*

Tevyn laughed out loud—belly laughed. *I'll take that under consideration.*

They texted some more, Mallory's drollness coming across in text as much as it did in person. Finally Tevyn shooed him off the phone so they could both get some sleep.

Missy woke up again shortly after that, calling for him.

"Tev? Tev, son—where'd you go?"

"Right here, Grandma. What's wrong?"

"Had a dream," she said, yawning to get more air. "Dreamt you were lost and all alone."

Tevyn thought of the last five years, the cheering in his ears, the lack of solid earth under his feet. "Weren't far off," he said.

"And a man was calling for you. And all you had to do was answer. You're gonna answer him, right?"

"Just did, Grandma."

"Good. I can sleep if you answer him. Night, Tevyn."

"Night, Grandma."

She fell back asleep, and he kissed her cheek.

It was the last time she woke up.

**MALLORY** got there at one in the afternoon, looking rumpled and harried and dear. Tevyn was sitting next to her bed, watching as her chest lifted gently and fell, a little less each time. A hospice nurse worked silent monitors behind them that measured her draining life in smaller and smaller increments of oxygen. He'd worked hard to be invisible, and Tevyn was grateful.

But not nearly as grateful as he was to see Mallory.

He stood as Mallory came in, then hugged him, hard.

"Tev? Is, uh—"

"Soon," he whispered. "Come sit." Mallory sat and pulled him into his lap, which was sort of a dick move from most guys taller than Tevyn, but with Mallory it was a bid to be closer.

And that's all he did. Hold Tevyn close as they sat for the next half hour.

"She told me you were calling for me," Tevyn whispered sometime in there. "Said I should answer."

"Yeah? What's your answer?"

"Yes."

"To what?"

"Anything you want. I'll give you anything. Just hold me. Hold me until…."

Mallory did exactly that, and Tevyn laid his head on Mal's shoulder and cried softly, until the last of the monitors went still, and she was gone.

And then—oh Mal—he did the most wonderful thing.

He sang a hymn, one Tevyn remembered from childhood, something so sweet and so simple the words came flowing back again.

Their voices stilled and the quiet in the room took over.

"Thanks, Mal."

"For what?"

"For staying."

How long was it? Two weeks? Was it really only two weeks ago? When he'd asked Mallory to stay?

And he had. He'd stayed through everything. Through a blizzard, through a reckless trip down a mountain.

For the most painful moment of Tevyn's life, this here, right now.

Tevyn would trust him to stay for everything else. It's how Mal was made.


**A WEEK** later they entered Missy's cabin practically limp with exhaustion.

Mal had been wonderful, helping to plan everything—funeral, flowers, donations to Missy's church. He'd contracted builders to come in and fix the cabin up come spring, and contracted someone to keep an eye on it in the winter while Tevyn finished up his itinerary. The service for Missy had been that morning, and Tevyn had stood up for his grandmother, thanking her friends, the people she'd spent most of her life with on this mountain, for coming to say goodbye.

Everybody had cried—but everybody had laughed too.

Melissa Moore, no middle name, had lived a good and full life. Tevyn had been fortunate to grow up in her home, with the support of her small mountain community, and he was well aware.

At the end of the service, during the reception, a woman older than Missy had approached him, nibbling on a chocolate chip cookie.

"Tevyn?" she said, smiling. "You look surprisingly good for a dead man."

Tevyn had smiled at her. "Mrs. Thompson. You look beautiful as always."

She waved him off, laughing at his flattery. She was eighty-five if she was a day, and her face showed a life well lived in the elements. "I'm going to miss her. But I'm sort of irritated too. All that gumption, and she couldn't have waited for me to go first?"

"Well, a gas heater, internet—you know Missy had to go first with everything," he said, because it was true. His grandmother's cabin might be sorely outdated, but she was a pioneer among her small township, and everybody knew it.

"Unfair of her," Mrs. Thompson told him gravely. Her eyes sought Mallory out as he stood by the refreshments, thanking the ladies of the church for providing. "That young man, did he come with you?"

There was no judgment in her face, merely simple curiosity.

"He's mine," Tevyn said with pride. Mallory in a dark suit, hair combed, lean cheeks finally filling out a little, was still a fine figure to behold. Tevyn couldn't believe it had taken him five years to ask that man to dance.

"Good. Missy's big fear was leaving you alone— you know that, right?"

Tevyn remembered her last words and nodded. "Yes, ma'am."

"No fears about the afterlife—I'm pretty sure if they tried to close the gate, she would have barged her way in."

She'd been prepared to barge her way into Mallory Armstrong's office, actually, but he'd welcomed them both with kindness and a smile.

"I think that's fair to say."

"So I'm glad you have a young man of your own. He seems very kind. What's he do?"

"He's a financier." It sounded strange to say—too highbrow for the likes of Tevyn and Missy. "I call him the money man."

"Well, isn't that fancy." She laughed softly. "Which is good. Because you were the crown jewel on Missy's life. She said that to me often enough. It's only right you have someone like that to call your own."

Tevyn nodded. "Yes, ma'am, I do."


**THAT** conversation came back to him now as they entered the cabin, and his heart warmed.

"Shall I make some soup?" Mallory asked, heading for Tevyn's room, where their stuff was. Tevyn had a double bed—barely big enough for two adults, but it was where they'd been sleeping.

But not much more than sleeping, because Tevyn's heart had been too full.

"Sure." Tevyn followed him with his eyes, predicting what he was going to do next. Loafers in the little corner he'd claimed as his—check. Dress socks off and in the dirty clothes corner of his suitcase—check. Suit jacket down his shoulders, laid out on the bed and waiting for the hangar—check. Slacks, down his legs, just the same—check.

By the time he'd gotten to his necktie, Tevyn had stripped his slacks and sweater off, leaving them in a crumpled heap on the floor. He'd kicked off his half boots and yanked off his necktie, and by the time he got to the bedroom, he'd unbuttoned his dress shirt enough to slide it over his head, and he dropped that on the faded carpet too.

"Tev—yn?" Mallory stopped in midcall as Tevyn circled his waist with his hands and shoved at his boxers.

Tevyn ground his need into Mallory's backside, standing on tiptoes so he could nibble at the back of Mallory's neck.

He growled and managed a whole goddamned word. "Now."

"Now?"

"Now."

Mallory turned in his arms and took his mouth, so hard, so voraciously, Tevyn was almost overwhelmed.

Almost.

Hands—everywhere. He reclaimed Mallory's skin, cupping his throat in the vee of his fingers and thumb, palming his chest from there down to the waistband of his boxers.

"Lay back," Tevyn commanded roughly.

"I was going to take care of you for once." Mallory offered a tentative smile, but Tevyn shook his head.

"This *is* taking care of me. Now naked! *Now*!"

Oh, bless him, he stripped off his boxers and pulled back the covers, crawling into bed and lying there, naked, propped up on his elbows to watch Tevyn rustle through his suitcase for the shaving kit.

"We're running low," Tevyn muttered.

"Well, it's a small bottle, and we had a big night."

Yes—yes, they *had* had a big night. They'd made love like they'd never have another chance, because Tevyn had thought his world would end when he walked out that door.

And part of it had. He'd miss his grandmother forever—she would *always* be the voice in his head telling him to get back up after he fell down, telling him he could do anything he put his mind to, telling him he mattered.

But he was *still here*. He was alive, and the man he loved was on that bed looking at him with big trusting eyes. Tevyn wanted every part of that he could get. He wanted to drink Mallory's touch in through his skin, and pleasure them both until their bodies were reduced to basic elements—oxygen and lust.

He wanted to prove he was alive, and he wanted Mallory right there with him.

Tevyn practically leaped onto the bed, kissing down Mallory's body, finding the traces of the marks he'd left there over a week ago and biting them again.

He wanted Mallory marked as his, for all time. No doubt, ever again.

Mallory submitted to his foray down his neck, his chest, his stomach, and to Tevyn's delight, he tried to hold in his noises again.

Tevyn sucked hard on the soft skin of his stomach and looked up as Mallory grunted, building a whine up in his throat that he was trying not to let escape.

"Give it up," he said after he'd released his mouthful with a pop.

"Give what—"

"You're trying to be quiet, Mal. I've heard you get loud. We're in a cabin in the middle of winter, miles from nowhere. We barely got an SUV down Missy's road. I got no idea how she made it for years in a Toyota Corolla. The only way I'm not gonna make you scream is if you bring the mountain down on top of us, and I'll still die happy."

"I'm not that loud," Mallory grumbled with dignity.

Oh, but he was. He was gloriously loud, uninhibited in bed in a way Tevyn had never guessed in real life. And he trusted all of that passion to Tevyn, and Tevyn wasn't going to let a single drop, a single grunt, a single moan go to waste.

"Not that loud?" Tevyn teased, licking the head of his cock. "Really?"

"Re—" His voice cracked, rising up an octave. "—*ally!*"

Tevyn took him all the way into the pressure and heat of his mouth, smiling on the inside when Mal hit the note above high C.

He kept sucking, kept teasing, until Mal was straining upward, shaking with need, and then he slid his boxers down his hips and grabbed the slick, drizzling some of the coolness onto Mallory's heated flesh.

Mallory caught his breath and looked at his own erection in surprise. "Uh—"

And then Tevyn caught his gaze and moved his own slippery fingers to his own backside. Cool and invasive and… ah….

Tevyn shuddered as he prepared himself, and fought against closing his eyes.

Mallory stared at him and licked his slightly parted lips. "Uh, should I—"

"Right there," Tevyn breathed, stretching, squatting to fill himself up. "Stay right there."

He straightened and pulled his fingers out, then straddled Mallory's hips, rising up above him and positioning his member right... oh yes... there.

And then he relaxed his thighs, his clench, and let the weight of his body pull him all the way down.

"Ah...."

Mallory gripped his thighs tightly, and as Tevyn hit bottom, he gave a long, drawn-out moan.

"Oh, Tevyn...."

"Mm... stay right there. Right... oh God. Okay. I'm gonna move." He leaned forward, body shaking with urgency and began to slide up and down, rocking forward and backward with Mallory embedded deeply inside. Oh! It was so good! So good! But he needed to go faster! Dammit, he needed to go—

Mallory locked his hands around Tevyn's waist and held him still, rocketing his hips up and down to pound inside Tevyn from the bottom, hard and fast, and Tevyn threw his head back and howled.

"Yes! God! Mal! Faster! Oh, man, please, harder! Faster! Wha—"

Mallory slammed Tevyn down on top of him and rolled until Tev was on his back, helpless, needy, and Mallory was doing what he did best.

Taking care of Tevyn.

He pumped, brutally hard until Tevyn's vision washed white and his orgasm rushed his spine. He grabbed his own erection and squeezed, needing the pressure, so lost in what Mallory was doing to his body, he had no shame and no embarrassment about the tables turning.

He needed, he needed, he needed, he needed oh— oh God—"*I need you right—fuck!—there!*"

Mallory buried himself inside Tevyn to the hilt and pumped hard and hot, scalding Tevyn with the force of his spend, and Tevyn erupted, spurting across his abdomen, his chest, his chin, catching a few drops in his parted mouth.

The taste of his own come set him off again.

Mallory groaned, so deep in his stomach that Tevyn could feel it where they were joined. Then he fell forward, taking Tevyn's mouth masterfully, kissing him until they were both limp and starving for breath.

"I thought *I* was loud," Mal breathed before dislodging himself from Tevyn's body to pull up the sheets and blanket and quilt from the foot of the bed. It was still Missy's place in February, and it was cold even after Mal had turned on the heater.

"C'mere," Tevyn begged, and Mal didn't disappoint him. He pushed up the bed, pulling the covers over their shoulders, and lying with his head on Tevyn's chest.

Ah, it was like he knew what Tevyn needed to do.

Tevyn stroked his hair and kissed the crown of his head.

"Still want that soup?" Mallory said with a laugh.

"Later." Tevyn kissed his forehead. "What next?"

"I thought there'd be soup."

He flicked the spot he'd just kissed. "No—I mean... *us*. What next?"

Mallory pushed up on his elbow and studied Tevyn's face. "Well, you have a competition in Toronto in two weeks. I assume you'll go up a few days before to try the course out, get loose."

Tevyn nodded, falling into his brown eyes in a way he'd never allowed himself to do before the crash. "Yeah. But before then?"

Mallory blinked. "Well, I figured we'd seal up the cabin and leave the key with the person we're paying to take care of it, and fly back to San Francisco. I commute to work, you can drive up to Sugar Bowl and practice if you need to. I mean, you usually stay in Aspen or Sugar Bowl anyway, between competitions, right?"

Tevyn nodded. "Yeah."

"So, when you need to, you go. When you don't—"

"I live with you," Tevyn said, smiling. Made so much sense. Of course Mallory had planned it that way.

"Yeah." It suddenly seemed to hit Mal, the enormity of what he'd said. "I… never mind. I could leave you here, and I'd see you at your next competition, and—"

Tevyn tilted Mal's face up so he could kiss him. He pulled back and licked his nose. "Don't you dare," he said firmly, laughing as Mal tried to decide whether he needed to defend himself or not. "Don't you dare change that amazing, awesome, wonderful plan. You can't make it to all my competitions, and you have other clients. I know that. But living in San Francisco and driving to train when I need to be on the slopes—I can do that."

"There's surfing in the bay, in wet suits," Mallory told him. "And in Santa Cruz."

Tevyn kissed him again. "And sometimes, you could come with me."

Mallory smiled, looking as happy as Tevyn had ever seen him. "I'd love that."

Tevyn sobered. "And I would only ever be with you. And you would only ever be with me."

"Yes."

"Because that's how it should have been all along."

Mallory looked away. "You needed time," he said.

"I took all the time I needed. I'm grown-up now, Mallory."

Mallory nodded, and Tevyn felt a stinging wetness against his chest. "What—oh my God, Mallory—"

"I'm happy," he whispered. "I'm sorry. I know you're grieving, and we just got down from the damned mountain, but I'm so happy—"

Tevyn kissed him, a teary sloppy disaster of a kiss that turned into Tevyn taking his turn inside Mal, pounding him until there were no more tears, only happy cries.

They would make it work the same way they'd made it down the mountain. One problem at a time, doing what they needed to stay together, never giving up.

Except the payoff wouldn't just be permission to exist from the elements—not this time. The payoff for navigating their relationship would be the promise of *life*.

## *Catching Great Air*

**"MALLORY,** c'mon, we have to go!" Damien urged, and Mallory took one more look around the office to make sure he got everything. He'd brought his luggage to work, and Damien had already carted most of it to the helipad on top of the building. "He expects you at the lodge tonight—you promised!"

"I'm coming! Charlie! We're leaving!"

"Aw, man! C'mon, Scooter! Let's go see the daddy!"

Mallory rolled his eyes. "How come Tevyn gets to be the daddy?"

"I have no idea. Now let's go."

The time trials to make the Olympic team were in Aspen. Damien was piloting them to the private airfield nearby so Glen could take them by company jet. It was good to have money—and friends who were pilots and willing to charter out to them so Mallory could leave the office for a solid three weeks and be at the Olympics with Tevyn.

But first, Tevyn had to qualify in Aspen so he could fly to Toronto, and Mallory had promised he'd be there.

Scooter came bounding into his office, dragging his lead behind him. Charlie followed, cursing good-naturedly at everybody's giant furry baby.

Preston had come through with a dog, getting a mix between Great Pyrenees, Great Dane, and basic Labrador retriever. The resultant litter had been fantastically big, extremely playful—and so sweet and mellow that with some training, Mallory had gotten Scooter certified as a service dog, and he and Preston took him to a local school for autistic students on the weekends Tevyn was gone and Mallory couldn't follow.

Scooter would let kids tug on his ears, his tail, his fur, and do nothing more than whine gently in rebuke if they got too rough.

And the children fell in love with him and told him things they were afraid to tell parents or teachers or other children. Mallory loved what kinds of magic the big dog could bring out of people, and Tevyn loved having a dog to watch after Mallory when he wasn't home.

He'd been gone for a week to train, and Mallory missed him. A lot.

"Mal, don't forget your knitting!" Charlie handed him the serviceable canvas bag that Tevyn had bought him for Christmas. They'd spent a month over the summer, deciding what to send to Mallory's little house in San Mateo and what to leave at the cabin or sell.

Mal—true to his word on the mountain—had taught himself to knit, and had taken all of Missy's knitting equipment and the stunning stash of yarn she had saved, most of it from a local mill in nearby Granby. After looking at the sweaters she'd knitted him and Tevyn, he'd asked some advice from a local yarn shop proprietress and started on a sweater of his own.

For Tevyn, of course.

If he knitted quickly—and blocked it in the hotel room that night—Tevyn would have it to wear at the trials—and later, at the Olympics.

For luck.

For love.

For knowing that another person in the world would do that for him, because Tevyn still needed to be told.

But Mallory didn't mind telling him.

Their lives were busy, chaotic, and tumultuous. But every time they could find to spend together was perfect, peaceful, and glorious.

And as often as he could, Mallory followed Tevyn up any mountain he needed to travel.

And as often as he could, Tevyn would stay in Mallory's arms.

Mallory hugged Charlie goodbye and got Scooter strapped into the company helicopter. He stayed in the passenger compartment to keep Scooter company, but he put on the headset because he hadn't talked to Damien in a couple of weeks and he wanted to catch up.

"So," he said carefully, "how's Preston?"

"You know better than I do," Damien replied, all sourness. "You have a dog. Mal has a dog, so Mal gets to talk to Preston. Damien's got jack, so Preston doesn't talk to Damien."

"No, but Preston talks *about* Damien all the time!" Mallory laughed. "Come on, Damie, ask the boy out! He's dying for you to! I mean, I know you've been called in on jobs before—don't you talk then?"

"Only about the job," Damien muttered. "Seriously, it's like he got all excited when we came down the mountain, but he saw me in the hospital, and I terrify him now. I don't get it."

"Maybe you have to ask him directly," Mallory told him. "Preston doesn't flirt, and he doesn't do sarcasm or innuendo. Tell him you want him."

"I'd probably have better luck if I got a dog."

"Well, I'm not going to argue. I really love Scooter!" Mallory hugged Scooter's neck and scratched his thick fur. "Yes, I do, Scooter boy. Yes, I do!"

"Do I need to sign off so you and Scooter can have private time?"

"No, sir. Keep telling me how you're going to ask Preston out on an actual date so I don't have to watch you mope for another year."

It hadn't been moping. Damien still walked with a limp—and it had taken a hard year of physical therapy and training to get to the point where he could walk without a cane. But they didn't talk about that because Damien didn't talk about that… because apparently Damien was a man's man who didn't admit that even this—going up in a helicopter in a relatively tame, urban setting—was terrifying.

For both of them.

Tevyn didn't get frightened—he said Mallory was all the grounding he needed.

But Mallory knew that for the rest of his life, taking a step onto any sort of aircraft was going to be an act of sheer will. He'd never told Tevyn, but getting on the plane for Colorado before Missy died had induced a full-blown panic attack in the bathroom beforehand. Tevyn hadn't realized until they'd flown home that some parts of them would always be on that mountain.

Scooter whined and licked his face. Calming Mallory down was his job too, and one of the reasons Mallory got to keep him when Tevyn was gone.

Tevyn wanted Mal to have someone to hold if he had to fly alone.

"You're mean," Damien said critically. "You weren't this mean on the mountain, Mallory. I would have remembered."

"You would not have!" Mal retorted. "We did our best to keep you as stoned as possible."

Damien chuckled. "It's true!"

They bantered all the way to the airfield, and when they got there, Damien hopped into the copilot cockpit and let Glen take over in the pilot's seat. Mallory and Scooter had the entire passenger compartment of the little twelve-seater to themselves, and Mallory knitted frantically and listened to e-books while Scooter rested his head on Mallory's knee.

The sweater was knitted all in one piece, like the ones Missy had made, and Mallory bound off the final stitches as the plane landed, and wove in the ends as Glen drove them through the snow to the ski lodge.

Damien took a look at his work as they piloted up the hill. "Nice. Almost exactly like the ones we wore."

"Missy used to make him one every year for competition season," Mal said. "For luck." Tevyn had missed his grandmother a lot in the last year. Mallory had worked so hard on the damned sweater while he'd been gone.

"*Very* nice." Damien nodded. "I'll take notes."

"Notes?" Glen snorted from the front seat. "You need to take a whole class. God, you're bad at courting."

"Says the man who hasn't been on a date since college!" Damien snapped back.

"Yeah, but I'm not looking at my little brother all cow-eyed and sad either."

"Thank God, because that would be gross."

"You know what I mean!"

Damien raised his eyebrows at Mallory to signal he was going in for the kill. "Yeah, you mean that you'd be just fine if I grabbed Preston by the hair and dragged him off to my gay cave because that's how *you* court men, but I think he deserves more than that!"

"It's a man cave," Glen snapped. "I may be gay, but the only thing gay about my cave is me!"

Mallory burst out laughing. "Give it up, Glen. Damien wins."

"He always fuckin' wins."

Damien and Mallory squeezed their eyes shut and tried not to laugh at Glen's out-and-out disgust. Glen and Damien's banter had gotten Mallory through as much traveling as Scooter's patient company. Tevyn said that was fine as long as Tevyn was the gold at the end of the run.

Mallory's heart was pounding at the thought of seeing Tevyn again.

Tevyn was always the gold at the end of the run.

He was waiting for them as they pulled up to the lodge, pacing outside in the heated patio, as excited as Scooter at the prospect of reunion.

Mallory swung open the door, and Damien told him, "Let the dog go first, Mal. Then I can take him for a poop walk, and we'll take our stuff up to the room."

Mallory was still struggling to Tevyn, yarn bag on his shoulder, loafers slick in the snow, as Tevyn and Scooter said their hellos. Scooter—who behaved for everybody *except* Tevyn—stood on his hind legs, put his paws on Tevyn's shoulders, and licked his face from scruffy jaw to eyebrows while Tevyn sputtered and laughed.

Finally Damien called, "Scooter! C'mon, boy! Uncle Damien's got a poop bag with your name on it!" Scooter disappeared, and it was just Tevyn and Mallory.

They paused for a moment, the last of the light falling across Tevyn's eyes, and he looked at Mallory like he hung the moon.

"You're here," he said, brushing Mallory's lips with his.

"Yeah."

"I'm so nervous—but you're here."

"Nervous?" Mallory laughed. Tevyn's confidence on the field since their little sleigh ride had been off the charts. The sports commentators described him as fearless—and Mallory watched him with his heart in his throat. "You're never nervous."

"I have something for you," Tevyn mumbled, burying his face in his shoulder. "They're doing a spotlight on us, if I qualify tomorrow. But before they do it, I wanted to give this to you and ask you the thing because if they do a spotlight on us and the whole world sees you, they need to see you like I see you."

"I have something for you too," Mallory said. "But other than that, I have no idea what you're talking about."

Tevyn looked up at him quickly. "You have something for me? You go first."

Suddenly Mal was swamped with embarrassment, but he reached gamely inside his knitting bag anyway and pulled out the sweater. Fine-gauge wool, simply made, Mallory had perfected his stitching by going around and around and around for a solid month of knitting while Tevyn had been training. "So you'd have one," he mumbled. "You know. For the competition. Because—"

Tevyn took it from him, fingering the colorful yarn and smiling softly. "Oh, Mal. This—this is perfect. You made this for me?"

Mallory grimaced. "Still not my colors." He still wore plain suits and sweaters of navy blue. Even Scooter was almost uniformly brown. The most colorful thing in his life was and always would be Tevyn.

But Tevyn didn't seem to care. He was petting the wool—which had a faint halo to it—and looking at Mallory dreamily. "You didn't even tell me you were working on it!"

He'd been there through Mallory's nascent attempts to learn the craft. He was wearing a mangled, hole-ridden disaster piece right now that was Mal's first attempt at a scarf.

"I didn't want to disappoint you," he said, absurdly touched by Tevyn's wonder. "I... she always made you one before competition season, and you're in the time trials tomorrow and the half-pipe, and I wanted you to know... you know. Someone in your corner."

Tevyn's eyes had grown shiny. "See!" he exclaimed, hugging the sweater to him. "That's what I'm talking about. Someone. Someone special. The network does a spotlight on all of the Olympic competitors. They air it on TV during breaks in the game coverage."

Mallory blinked. "Yeah! I know those!" It was how he first fell in love with snowboarding as a kid. How he'd first known to look for a Tevyn Moore when he walked into Mal's life. "They're doing one on you?"

"Yeah," Tevyn said. "And they wanted to know about the crash. And they kept saying, 'So, you're still seeing Mallory Armstrong,' and I was like, 'We're living together,' and they were like, 'So it's serious?' and it was making me mad."

"Mad?" Oh, that couldn't be good.

"Because I'm not just *seeing* you. You're my *life*. You're my foundation. When I get down the hill, I want to share the run with you. When I come to train, I'm always weighing is the time on the mountain worth the time I'm missing with you. And sometimes it is, but sometimes it isn't, and that's a real thing. And when I'm with you, it's like a really beautiful run, all the time. There's this absolute joy when I see you."

"Why would that make you mad?" Oh, Mallory was so lost. The last of the sun disappeared, leaving Tevyn's eyes begging him in the twilight to understand.

"Because saying 'I'm *seeing* you' isn't enough!" Tevyn burst out. "I want to be *married* to you!" He rummaged in his pocket and pulled out a little box. "These are silicone so I can wear mine on the slopes. But I want to pick out gold ones, like, Black Hills gold, with all the color, and I want to wear those in the city. And I want us to have the ceremony and everything and wear them. And when someone's interviewing me about the guy who followed me down the mountain because he believed in me and had faith in us, I want them to be talking about my husband, not some guy I'm seeing. I want us to get married, Mallory. After the Olympics. As soon as possible. I'd take during the Olympics or before them if I could, but I'm shit at planning, so that's going to be on you. Because you plan the dreams and together we live them, right? So could you plan a wedding for us, Mallory Armstrong, whose middle name I still don't know? Would you marry me?"

"Clarence," Mallory said through a dry throat. "Yes, Tevyn Simmons Moore, I, Mallory Clarence Armstrong, want to marry you on top of a mountain, just like this one, right when the sun sets, so the whole world can see you're the light of my life."

His face was wet, the chill of the evening freezing the tears on his cheeks, and he didn't care. He lowered his head to Tevyn's because not kissing him then would be unthinkable.

In the background they heard Scooter barking and Damien calling after him, and when the kiss was over, Mallory would start the planning, think about how to marry Tevyn Moore after the Olympics, on top of a snowy mountain, with all of their friends around as well as their giant dog.

Think about how to tell the world that love was always worth the risk, and that faith could be rewarded, and that whether you stayed on the mountain or came down, what mattered was you did it together.

After the kiss was over, he'd think about this.

Right now, Tevyn's mouth on his, their hearts overwhelmed and overflowing, Tevyn was the only thing he could think about. Tevyn who was Mallory's heart, just as Mallory was his.

# Coming in August 2019

## DREAMSPUN DESIRES

**Dreamspun Desires #87**
**Small Town Sonata** by Jamie Fessenden

Can the trusted town handyman rebuild a broken pianist's heart?

When a freak accident ends Aiden's career as a world-renowned classical pianist, he retreats to his New Hampshire hometown, where he finds the boy he liked growing up is even more appealing as a man.

Dean Cooper's life as handyman to the people of Springhaven might not be glamorous, but he's well-liked and happy. When Aiden drifts back into town, Dean is surprised to find the bond between them as strong as ever. But Aiden is distraught over the loss of his career and determined to get back on the international stage.

Seventeen years ago Dean made a sacrifice and let Aiden walk away. Now, with their romance rekindling, he knows he'll have to make the sacrifice all over again. This time it may be more than he can bear.

**Dreamspun Desires #88**
**Beauregard and the Beast** by Evie Drae
A Once Upon a Vegas Night Tale

His greatest prize can't be won in the octagon.

Champion MMA fighter Adam Littrell needs no distractions as he prepares for the fight that will determine whether he retires. But when he opens the door of his swanky Las Vegas home to his new personal assistant, Bo Wilkins, staying focused becomes a struggle.

Aware of Adam's surly reputation, Bo doesn't expect to like his new employer, let alone fall for him. But Bo is pleasantly surprised when a shared love of books leads them to study for their GEDs together and plan for a life after their current careers. Adam won't be able to fight forever, and Bo wants a relationship on equal footing.

But just as their relationship is getting off the ground, the sister Bo raised needs his help, and he drops everything. With Adam's final match looming and Bo in a different city, reuniting will be the real challenge.